SELINA

SOMYA JAIN

Made with ♥ on the Notion Press Platform
www.notionpress.com

Contents

Contents

Preface

Selina began as a completely different story than seen in this book however, twenty chapters in I realised that aliens and space fiction were not what Selina needed. What she needed was a bit of Indian Mythology, some dystopian elements and lots of action. So here it is, the story that I believe Selina would enjoy as her life and I hope you will enjoy too!

Acknowledgements

I would like to thank my parents,
Mrs Reena Jain and Mr Sandeep Jain,
without whose encouragement the book would never
have been completed!

I

One

Grief is such an inexplicable emotion. It strikes you suddenly, just like a predator in the dense forests of Gionia, at a moment when you least expect it to hit you, to deflate you like a balloon, to suck the life out of you, to make you feel like nothing ever mattered because no matter what you did, its all just a memory now, a memory that will stay with you until you die and you are lost into oblivion.

I didn't expect to feel so shattered, so lost, so suffocated in my homeland but ever since that day, I do. The rivers and the mountains that called out to me once upon a time, scare me like a nightmare on a cold, Hutata night.

Oh, how we used to joke around every Hutata, make fun of our ancestors for being so foolishly afraid of creatures that don't exist, and yet here we are.

I remember her pranking everyone last year by saying that she had seen a vivid, yet beautifully horrid dream on a Hutata night, the sheer panic on the tribe's face was worth a hundred photographs but the elders had not seen the humour in it and had locked her in that terrible place called Thornos, for two whole months.

When she came out, she wasn't the same. She had been abused and broken, her spirit had been sucked out and all she ever said was that she could see things happening- horrendous creatures, wars, death and destruction. These were all that she ever talked about but no one believes you once you have been called out and no one believed her except me.

And yet, what a terrible friend I am-was, that I couldn't see her pain, the truth behind her words, couldn't leave a school day to go with her to the place she had been constantly mentioning for a whole week, and now- now I can only repent. The ifs haunting me despite knowing better.

As I climb up, ignoring the panic surging through my body, I can't help but reminisce about that fateful day that changed my life forever.

Two months back...

'Selina, they are coming, he has sent them here to take revenge, to destroy us all, and they are coming. Their leader is vengeful, he is ready to take revenge on us all for things we have not done. This time he won't stop Selina, we have to go there and delay them, we have to go there tomorrow.' Rosa said, her eyes going crazy, fingers shaking and feet tapping on the ground in a rhythm unknown.

Rosa was a beautiful girl. Her red hair fell down to her waist in cascades, her blue eyes reminded one of the oceans far away and her skin had a beautiful pale glow on the days she took a bath but these days the fear that was gnawing at her heart deterred her from doing anything at all. The voice had told her that she would die but she didn't believe it for a second. No one could kill her when she had her best friend at her back. Even when those monsters were taking her away, Selina had fought with them, until they had beaten her black and blue. She had even tried to rescue her from hell, but they had threatened to capture her father. That was when Rosa had subtly asked her to stop all her futile attempts that would cause more damage than good.

On the day of being released, Selina had defied authorities and worn a gaudy shade of pink to welcome her. Though she had received her first black dot, that day, nothing could make her gloomy. She had smiled her toothy grin despite knowing that just two more dots and she would be killed in front of the whole tribe.

'Rosa, I will go with you, but only after school ends. You know how my Ma gets when I miss school. She wouldn't scold me for being rebellious about other stuff, but school-school is a temple for her that I need to visit everyday. I will finish all the homework in the school itself, then sneak some food from the house and we will set on this adventure you want to go to so desperately, alright?' Selina said, the sudden breeze causing a few strands of her dry, black hair to fall onto her face.

Unlike Rosa, Selina didn't have any special coloured eyes, they were plain black but despite that, they were beautiful. Her long lashes made up for the excess of melanin in her irises and her lightly brown skin always glowed in the golden hour before the sunset.

'But Selina, we need to reach there before sunset, and we can't do that if you go to school. Please miss a day, I will convince Aunt Urusa. Please Selina, please!' Rosa nearly cried, the voice growing louder in her ears, mocking her for expecting her best friend to give up everything to go do what- stop those monsters that everyone knew didn't exist!

'Rosa-Rosa are you okay? I think you need some more rest, Rosa, you need to sleep and you definitely need to take a bath. Come, take a shower at my house, have a hot meal and sleep in my room tonight. When with me, nothing will scare you. Common, you take rest till tomorrow then we will leave the minute I return, okay?' Selina asked, worried about her friend who had suddenly gotten a ghostly shadow on her face.

Rosa nodded ever so slightly that any other person would have missed it completely but Selina knew.

She wished she could beat up those terrible elders for what they had done to her friend but she was only sixteen. If she behaved like that, they would hurt her parents first and then come for her. So she rebelled by doing everything to make them angry but within limits to leave them aching to punish her.

She wore dresses with hints of bright colours that could not be held for acts of hate towards the leaders, she practiced using a Gun everyday but did not keep one at home, she ran like girls weren't supposed to but only at a speed higher than walking so they couldn't catch her for wrongly influencing other minors. She was defiant in every way but knew her boundaries.

Selina gently took hold of her best friend's hand and helped her get up. She further went on to keep her free hand around Rosa's shoulder to keep her from falling. The punishment had made Rosa excruciatingly weak and it broke her heart to see her beautiful friend struggling like that.

Once they reached home, her mother who adored Rosa like her own, made Rosa's favourite meal, Paneer Pulao, for her but the girl couldn't eat more than two bites.

Urusa looked at the young girl with sympathy. Once she had finally bathed and settled next to Selina, Urusa gave both the girls a good night kiss and said a little prayer in her mind to keep them safe before herself retiring for the night.

When Selina woke up the next day, Rosa was still sleeping, little did she know that the girl was awake and planning to leave as soon as Selina left. In fact, she had been up the entire night. The voice had told her if she brought Selina along, the latter would die a torturous death.

School was dreadfully boring and by the time Selina came back brimming with excitement for the adventure, Rosa was nowhere to be found. She had left in the morning to go back to her house but Selina knew her friend. She immediately started for Jakota Hills, the place Rosa wanted to go to and what she found there, terrified her for life.

Next to the valley of River Fiona, was a pool of fresh blood and in it she found Rosa's dress. Soaked red, and torn to bits like it had seen a fight. She never found Rosa's body but the trail of something being dragged into the river made it obvious that Rosa had been dragged inside. She immediately jumped into the cold water to look for her friend but other than catching a bad cold, she found nada, absolutely nothing.

The tribe refused to look for a crazy girl and Rosa's mother couldn't care less about her only daughter. The only person who helped her was her mother but what could a woman and a little girl even find in a huge countryside?

Since that day, Selina had spent everyday searching for her friend but two months later, a fisherman she had befriended had found a finger, one Selina could identify anywhere and it destroyed her.

II
Two

The sun gleams in my eyes as I look up to see how far I have to make before I can collapse for a while. Ever since that day, I have made it my life's mission to go to every place Rosa had mentioned in those months after her release. What if I was mistaken, what if she is still alive, waiting for me to find her?

The Khol mountains are located on the outer boundaries of our village, Kholali. They are a long chain with the highest peaks covered in snow. Most people are afraid to venture to its southern borders which are near the Tooth village, whose black magicians are famous far and wide for their cannibalistic habits, but the northern hills are great picnic spots.

Despite everything, Polki Peak is an exception to the other peaks in the northern part of the range. Ever since fourteen children died there many years before I was born, people have considered Polki to be haunted. Except for one or two brave hearts who sometimes climb up here during mid-summer to collect the Ghishu plant which has excellent healing properties, no one comes here.

Climbing up with all my might, I almost fall, when a huge chunk of rock suddenly slips from the top and nearly knocks me out. Holding on with all my might and ignoring the sharp pain in my left hand from the injury caused by the rock, I continue climbing up with my teeth clenched.

Why in the world did Rosa want to come up here? Everytime Rosa mentioned this place, there was a gleam in her eyes, she was almost her old self but whenever she would be about to tell me the reason for coming here, something would disturb us. Her reason, her story, and her excitement all went along with her, leaving me all alone to explore and find the whys.

Finally, after a million years- twenty minutes, I reach the top. Hoisting myself up with all the little energy left in my tiny body, I fall onto the soft grass with a thud. I roll onto my back once the impact wears out and sit up slowly to find myself staring at the most beautiful piece of land I have ever seen. My hand still hurts but once I gulp down the pain medicine in my bag, I feel fine in a minute.

There is a peace on this peak that I haven't felt since Rosa di- went missing. The breeze is gentle and cool, and the trees on the other side are gently swaying as if dancing to the tunes of the loving air. There are flowers of literally every colour in the fields and the grass is fresh and green like someone has pulled out all the weeds.

The whole place looks like a well-maintained garden similar to those I had once seen in the big bungalows in Sehar. Sehar, our capital, the place where are royals stayed, where Slice stays. How would he react if he got to know that Rose was tortured, that she had suffered like no one and now that she had- she had gone missing, no one had even bothered to search for her? I was afraid of calling him, even though I didn't know how to contact him, for I knew his anger would spare no one if I told him.

Trub was the only one who could control Slice. He was the brains of our group but now he lives in Tooth village and we can never contact him again by any means. How great would it have been if we were never separated at twelve, if we could still be together, then Rosa would be here too, because where Rosa went Slice did too and he would never let anything happen to her, ever.

A tear slips from my eyes, then another and before I know I am sobbing. Every emotion that I had locked up, comes out as I realise how lonely I am without Rosa, how I have failed her as a friend. How can I ever face Slice again and Trub, that is if we ever meet again? I hate the system, if not for it, they all would be with me.

We are all born in Sehar, live there until we turn twelve, make friends, learn the fundamentals and then we are sent back home as if we are some emotionless monsters who wouldn't feel a pang in their hearts on being separated from our loved ones. I always considered myself lucky to have met Rosa, at least she was there with me when we had to come back. Slice was stuck in that brooding, rule-abiding castle and Trub, went back right before Tooth village was declared to be a forbidden place of the kingdom.

I often wonder what life would have been like before the Great Climatic Revenge when there were no such kingdoms, when there was technology and when there were no such pathetic rules.

Wiping away my tears hastily, I take deep breaths to calm the anxiety building in me and stand back up to survey the place. There is no sign of life other than the plants. I had often thought there would be dacoits living here and they must be the ones scaring everyone away but now I am lost. What is it about this beautiful place that's scary?

I walk around, carefully sniffing the flowers and examining the soil, until I reach the trees. They are tall and dense. Everything about the trees feels wrong and my gut tells me to run but I am Selina Stardrew and I am not a coward. Leaving the bright land, I start walking inside the canopy formed by the trees, with my senses on high alert to be careful of the wild animals and reptiles that are often roaming around in forests. As I walk deeper into the jungle, the sunlight dims completely and it feels like a dark, moonless night.

As I turn around to go back into the lighted area, suddenly, my foot lands on a strange, pebbled surface and within a second I find myself hanging upside down from a branch. My scream gets stuck in my throat as something slides up my body and wraps around my throat. I freeze. What did I land myself into? Goosebumps cover my hands and I feel dizzy with fear. Is this how I will die?

Suddenly the wind speeds up, sounding almost like a little child learning how to whistle.

'A power looms to take revenge, a voice to misguide the best, an army of soon to be dead, a leader to guide her friends.'

Wait what was that? Did I hear it right or the wind did say something? No no no, how can the wind speak? The coil around my neck suddenly loosens and kind of helps to put me back to the ground.

As soon as my feet touch the floor of the mighty jungle, I run back towards the light, the strange words ringing in my ears. How is it possible, how can wind speak? I am surely growing crazy. The grief is finally turning me insane, yes that's what it is.

The sun is almost setting once I see the flowers again and I run to the side I think I came from to get down at once. Immediately setting up my ropes I start climbing down again and in less than half the time I took to climb up, I find myself at the foot of the hill, running back to my house.

I nearly forget to lower my pace until I hear the siren of the officials and it is only then that I walk casually to my house, unaware of the trouble that has stirred in my uninformed absence.

My mother sits there, her head in her hands while the neighbours try to calm her down. My father stands near the door talking to an official about something. As soon as they see me, my mother walks up to me and hugs me tight.

What's wrong, why does she seem so relieved to see me? My father exchanges a few more words with the official before they leave along with the neighbours.

'What happened Ma? You have never been so nervous before of me returning late?' I ask, my voice laced with worry about things I don't know.

'A girl's body was found today. Her face was unrecognisable but she had a frame and hair like yours. You were missing and we couldn't help but assume the worst since no other girl we know has hair like yours in this village.' My mother says, her voice quivering and tears falling down her eyes. Papa also hugs me surprisingly before helping Ma calm down.

As I settle into bed that night, I can't help but feel that I am being watched. The words I had heard ring in my head and for the first time in a while, I fall asleep.

III

Three

I walk towards the flowers, surprised to see myself finding my way back to the peak. The blue roses captivate me and I can't help but run towards them. People love red and pink flowers but blue, blue is such a magnificent colour, it's peaceful, like a cool breeze on a hot summer day and on roses it's like a treasure, something to be adored and kept safely, not plucked and given as a gift.

I can't help but look at a particular rose closely that has petals that look like a royal blue shaded from bottom to top, dark to light as if representing the fact that you can rise from darkness to be fly in the vast horizons of the sky.

I bend a little closer to it, to smell its fragrance but as soon as I close my eyes, a sound makes me freeze.

Buzzzzz-buzzzz-buzzz...

Slightly opening my eyes, I see a huge bee coming out of the flower that suddenly doesn't look as pleasant as it did a few minutes back. Wherever the bee has touched the flower, it's turning a sickly shade of green, letting out a pungent smell. I try to run, but my feet don't move, I try to scream but no sound comes out. I have never been afraid of bees but it's different when you are paralysed.

My body is there but it just doesn't listen to me, like my soul has been detached from it and I am seeing a slow-motion film where I am going to be bitten by a huge, wild, poisonous bee.

As I prepare myself for the sting, something pushes me and I land in the forest. I look around for the force, struggling to get up when I am pushed again. I land in front of a castle this time. It's huge but well hidden by the trees.

As I try to stand up again, looking around for what has brought me here, I hear a whooshing sound and bend down just in time to avoid an arrow. A young girl, about my age, comes out running, her short blonde hair sticking to her face, her orange tunic too short like a men's shirt and her trousers bunched up on her feet. She runs past me to pick up the arrow.

Either she doesn't notice me or just doesn't care because as soon as she collects her arrow, she runs back without sparing me a glance.

As I contemplate whether to go back or not, she returns, this time accompanied by two other girls. One has dark skin, like people of Greog village usually have, and long black hair tied in a pleat. She is dressed in a grey tunic similar to the blondie but with trousers that actually fit her while the other is pale with red hair. Her appearance makes me freeze. No, it can't be her. It's not Rosa, no! But everything stills when I look at her face because she is indeed my best friend, my Rosa, the girl I have been searching for all this time, refusing to believe that she is dead.

They walk towards me but it's like I am invisible.

'Rosa, look at me, I am here. I am here to take you back.'

I try to scream but again no words come out. As if sensing my presence, she turns towards me with a frown but before she can contemplate more, I am pushed again and this time the place is not so happy. Fire flows like a river beside me, the heat making me flinch from the intensity. Sweat pours down my forehead as I wonder what I am doing here when I hear a chant.

'Long live the King, Long live the Master!'

How do people live here? I move forward, wondering at my luck. I can move here but a few minutes back my body was refusing to obey my brain. The rebels have now surrendered and I can walk normally. What even is going on?

As I walk closer to the sound, the chants become louder and there is a vibration, on the dusty, semi-cemented road, that goes all the way up to my head.

From my position, I see huge walls with fresh leaves hanging out. How in the world did they manage to get fresh leaves in this place? I can hardly see anything past about a hundred-two hundred meters and there is definitely no vegetation. When there is no water how will there be plants? I am pretty sure I am deep inside a mountain but how and why would someone choose to live here? Even the air is polluted and it's getting harder to breathe by the second.

'End of Earth, end of nasty humans, revenge from the Gods!'

Suddenly the chants change and I am left even more shocked. What do they mean by the end of humans?

I run towards the walls, and seeing a small opening that is big enough for me to enter, I crouch down and crawl past it to land on a big veranda with hundreds of guests and a stage, only the guests are not humans. I mean they are humans but they are huge. Even the smallest ones are at least ten times larger than the tallest humans I have seen.

They are eating leaves from small tree branches and some sea animals, that no humans would ever touch, with a glass of what I hope is wine.

On the stage, there are just two creatures. One is a giant who seems like the king due to a huge chunk of gold bar on his head, which is supported by pearls that have been used like pins, and a shiny red robe that can cover an entire village. The other looks like a human from my position, considering he is really small, like an ant next to an elephant, how I can see him is a wonder in itself.

Wait, I can't assume the gender of these creatures, maybe I should just use it till I find out.

The human-like creature is wearing a bright yellow robe that hurts my eyes and its face is not visible under the robe but despite this, it has a dangerous aura.

The other giants are dressed in everyday human clothes and have long matted hair decorated with colourful beads. It's funny to see so much colour in a lifeless place like this but how can I even comment? I live in a colourful world where bright clothes are not allowed and they live in hell where they use an extra dose of colour.

'We will attack in exactly twenty days. Our first target will be-'

What? Right before I can hear the name of the place, I am jolted out of the veranda once again to land in my village. It's quiet despite daytime and though it feels good to come out of a hell-like place full of weird creatures conspiring to take revenge, the eerie silence bugs me.

I move closer to the houses but there is no one in sight. Step by step I move closer to my house, in hopes of asking my mother where everyone is but there is no one in my house too.

I run out to the centre of the village, to the meeting point and my eyes pop out by the blood bath I see. My neighbours, classmates, and even my parents are lying there, their heads bleeding profusely. Even the elders, the people supposed to protect us, and govern us, the very ones I hate for the cruelty, are lying there, their eyes wide open like whatever they saw shocked them beyond measure.

I run to my mother, cradling her body in my arms, trying to wake her up, but nothing happens. She is dead. How did this happen?

'Selina, this is just a glimpse of what may happen if you continue to ignore your responsibilities. I have shown you where you need to go to stop the incoming war. Wake up and fulfil your destiny.'

I still on hearing the voice. It's feminine, soft and angelic like music.

'Who are you? Reveal yourself.'

I say standing up and looking around.

'In time, but tomorrow, you will have to clear your first task to prove that you have been rightly chosen by the fates.'

The voice says and before I can probe more, my eyes open and I find myself in bed, the first rays of the Sun coming through my window, proving the fact that it was all just a dream.

IV
Four

Why can't a teenager just live in peace for a day? As much as my Ma was scared yesterday, today she was persistent that I go to the weekly fair and help out my aunt Yursulana with her stall.

Every week, women in the community who worked in the fields near the Fiona riverbed, sold some unique items like shells, special stones, food items, fufu grasses, ancient findings and anything and everything that one couldn't imagine finding on their own. Rosa loved the strawberry candy stall and would eat so many candies of different shapes, sizes and fillings, that for the next two days she would only complain of stomach ache.

My aunt Yursulana, however, was a tarot reader. She liked to pretend that she knew magic, that she could predict the future.

After yesterday's dream, I had half a mind to go back to Polki Peak and find out if there was a castle but the thought of actually finding it scared me too since that meant my dream was real and there were really some Giants looking forward to end the world; the other half of me just wanted to go check if Rosa was actually there and who those other two girls were. The idea itself was much better than spending an entire day listening to my aunt spooking out the community's superstitious folks and earning a great fortune.

Other than every other worry clouding my mind, there was one more question that was eating me away, who was the girl who was killed yesterday and where was she from?

As I near the fair, the smell of popcorn, candies and even scented candles wafts through the air and combined with the chitter-chatter of the ladies and the playful screams of the younger teenagers, who are playing hula-hoops, it makes me want to run away.

I feel guilty for getting to experience everything without my best friend. She was the one who loved this place, who interacted with everyone with a huge smile on her face, and yet these women didn't waste a second to turn their backs on her when she needed their support. I clench my fists suddenly feeling angry at everyone. A part of me wants to give them a piece of my mind but I know better than to waste energy on people who don't deserve it. Besides Rosa would expect better from me.

My aunt's van is located near the far end of the fair, decorated with flowers, beads, and posters displaying the charges of the various services she provides. Today, she has gone a mile ahead and also put incense sticks in one corner and hung some cards with scary faces on the other.

A woman or two hang around the van, gathering the courage to speak to my aunt for she is not an easy woman. Unlike my mother, who looks all sweet and feminine with her black hair always hanging loose on the shoulders and her face youthful and pretty, my aunt looks scary and a hundred years old despite being only a year older than my ma. Smoking has made her voice heavy and combined with the kohl lines she makes around her eyes and on her forehead, she looks like the witch she claims to be.

Once I reach the van, I take a seat on one of the little chairs placed near the door and take a moment to look around. The joy on everyone's faces doesn't even give a hint of the officials surrounding the fair, their guns ready to shoot anyone who breaks the rules and creates havoc, their eyes watching for any unusual display of the smallest form of rebellion by the women, as if any of these women would even dare to do that.

We are allowed to be happy just not ecstatic enough with everything at the tips of our fingers to create a ruckus that can once again lead to events that angered nature years back.

The door to the van opens a few minutes later, and my aunt steps out in a black skirt and blouse, her long hair dyed a muddy brown shade and her haunting makeup in place. She asks me to clean up her van without sparing me a glance and immediately gets to business with the women who have finally taken a seat on the small chairs, ready to waste their money on bluff.

I hate cleaning the van, it's one thing to look at the weird cards, and magic items but to be actually touching them, no way! The door shuts on its own once I enter and I find myself face to face with a little black cat.

She looks at me like she is the employer who is going to give me wages for cleaning up the mess. Food cans, dry leaves and cigarettes are littered everywhere. I start by picking up the big wrappers and cans and filling them up in a white cloth bag, followed by sweeping and making the bed.

By the time I am done, I can't move a muscle. Who knew cleaning a small van would be such a task? When I step out for lunch, my aunt's table is hustling and bustling with crowds and so I decide to take lunch at the back of the van. The fair is located close to the Gionia forests and my aunt's van looks like the border that you need to cross to go inside.

I am busy stuffing my mouth with spoonfuls of rice when I see a shadow behind a tree.

'Who's it?' I call out but get no reply. Putting the bowl aside, I stand up to inform my aunt but decide otherwise. Carefully stepping on the grass, I go near the tree, but the shadow is now behind another one, a little further away. How did the person move so fast that I couldn't even see it?

I once again move towards it, but it moves further away. In no time, without realising it, I am deep inside the forest with no clue of where I came from. The light is dim because of the trees and I can't believe what a fool I have been to have followed a mere shadow that could have been caused by the sunlight.

I turn around to go back but something strikes me and I fall on my back. A huge man stands above me with a smirk on his face and his sword that's glinting from the little light falling on it, raised to kill me.

I gain senses just in time to roll over when he brings down the sword.

'Who are you?' I ask panting as I stand up to get a better look at my enemy. He looks like a mini giant, his hair and clothing like what I had seen the Giants wearing in my dream and his sword as huge as a branch of a tree.

'I am your death. No prophecy can stop us this time. I will end all girls with black hair.' He bellows before charging at me again.

I once again sidestep him, quickly realising his weakness.

'So you killed the other girl? Where did you bring her from?' I ask as he turns around to charge at me again.

'The Greog village, where else? Now stop wasting my time and get ready to die.' He says, this time coming faster than before and though I manage to avoid the sword, I trip on a root and fall sideways. He doesn't spare a second to hit me but I roll away quickly desperate to stay alive.

All the movement combined with the fall makes me dizzy but a plan forms in my brain. I may not have a gun, but using it has taught me how to aim. Collecting a few stones lying around me, I get up quickly and run to a distance from the baby Giant. He tries to catch up with me but his weight, combined with the trees in the way, holds him back.

Adrenaline shoots through me as I aim my first stone. The Giant is so lost in catching me that he doesn't even notice when my stone flies in his direction and pierces one of his eyes. Huge drops of blood splotch on the grass as he groans in pain. Fueled by agony he once again tries to catch me and cut me into two halves, this time with more intensity but anger can never help you. I run away once again and the minute he turns towards me, I hit him with another stone, making him blind.

While he falls down in pain, I continuously hurtle stones at his eyes, his agony filled screams shake the forest floor until eventually the brutal pain takes his life.

I don't understand the severity of my actions until the deed is done, and it's only after it that I come back to my senses and realise that I am a murderer.

The adrenaline goes away, and I slowly move back to where I think I came from, until the van is in sight but just before I can make it, I feel my eyes closing against my will.

V
Five

Cold water splashes on my face, waking me up with a jolt. I slowly open my eyes to see my aunt standing next to me with a pail of water in her hands and let out a groan both from pain and being woken up in such an awful manner.

'Hurry and get up before someone realises you were in the forest and change your clothes too! I don't get how you got so dirty, what were you doing killing someone out there?' My aunt says and suddenly everything comes flashing back to me. The giant, his confession of killing that girl, my self-defence that went a little too far, ok, way too far.

Will anyone believe me if I told them that I had killed a giant today, that too without any proper weapons? My entire body hurts and it's only when my aunt assists me that I am able to get up. She lets me into her van from the door facing the forest, to avoid everyone's attention and gently cleans the wounds, I don't remember getting. Once I am all clean, she gives me some clothes to change into and I am only halfway through when someone knocks at the door.

'Open up, monthly checking time!' A man says from outside and before I can panic my aunt pushes me onto the bed and covers me with a quilt. She then throws the blood-stained cotton and clothes into a small lamp which swallows them all to my horror before combing her hair with her hands and opening the door.

I close my eyes, pretending to be asleep as someone walks into the van, bumping their head on the roof.

At times I forget that the van is not exactly made for tall folks. The reminder of the word tall once again fills my head with the image of the dead giant and I can't help but feel remorse over my actions. He was a murderer but did he deserve to die by my hands?

It was an act of self-defence. A part of my brain says but the other part knows that I could have run after hurting him in one eye, there was no need to kill him.

'Why is she sleeping right now?' A deep voice says, bringing me out of my thoughts.

'She spent the entire morning cleaning my van and before that the entire week attending school, you know kids get tired after that.' My aunt says in a tone I have never heard her use before. Today my aunt is in a suspiciously good mood, which makes her scarier, to be honest.

'Fair enough, but if I get another complaint of her being up to no good, you and her are both going to be dead.' He says in a gruff voice before banging on the door on his way out I hope.

Who called the officers on me? Who was lingering around the forests to notice me going inside?

'Get up and go home, it's not safe anymore, and don't come to help me next week.' My aunt says, throwing the quilt away and pulling me up.

'No Aunty, you need to tell me what's going on? Who saw me? And what is that lamp?' I ask holding her hands tightly but she just pushes me out of the van before locking the door and quickly driving away, leaving me standing there all alone.

A few ladies snicker on seeing me left behind, but quickly mask their expressions when I glare at them.

Walking all the way home gives me a lot of time to sort my thoughts but I can't. Giants are real, my aunt has a lamp that swallows everything despite the size, and someone is keeping an eye on me for some reason.

When I reach home, I see my mother standing at the door, with her hands crossed. The minute she sees me, she ushers me inside and closes the door. For the first time, I see that the curtains are closed too and my father is back home early from work.

'Selina, take a seat.' Huh, do they know everything?

I sit down on a chair opposite my father who has worry etched on his face. My father is a huge man, but despite his exterior, he is a softy on the inside.

'Selina, what did you see in the forest today.' My mom jumps straight to the point. Who knew my aunt would be so quick at reporting things?

'Ma how-' I start but my father interrupts me.

'Selina, your aunt called a few minutes back. You can trust us.' He says and it does make sense but will they believe me?

'I- uh- I saw a shadow and followed it into the forest foolishly and it was- it wasagiantthatwantedtokillme.' I say and my parents look at me confused.

'Say it slowly, what was the shadow?' My Ma says while my Dad sits up straighter and moves to the edge of his seat.

'It was a giant that wanted to kill me, he confessed to killing the girl from yesterday.' I say and my Ma almost screams in shock.

'WHAT? WHERE IS IT NOW, WHO HELPED YOU? WE MUST THANK THAT PERSON.' Ma screams but she stills on seeing my expression.

'Someone helped you right? Where did the giant run, in which direction I mean.' She says while my Dad just looks at me in realisation.

'Urusa, I think it's enough for tonight. She needs to rest.' He says but my mother refuses to listen.

'I killed him mother.' I say and the gravity of the words fills the room with a strange fear.

'You-how-you are just a child.' My Ma says, following on the mat next to my chair.

'Adrenaline perhaps, he was intent on killing me and I had no other option so I used stones to blind him and then kept hurling stones at his eyes till he died from pain.' I say, tears falling from my eyes. My Dad gets up and hugs me while my Ma just sits there in shock.

'No-no no, it's happening Kirst. It's happening, our daughter, the prophecy-' my Ma starts saying but one look from my Dad and she immediately stops.

'What's happening, Ma, Papa, what's happening?' I say in between my sobs. Prophecy?

'*A power looms to take revenge, a voice to misguide the best, an army of soon to be dead, a leader to guide her friends.*'

The words suddenly ring in my head and I gulp, audibly. What if the words were true? What if the wind was trying to tell me that I was going to die?

'I think Dad is right, I should just go off to sleep.' I say but Ma stops me.

'You know the prophecy, don't you? Don't even think of lying because I am your mother and I can read your face.' She says getting up and despite my Dad trying to interfere, I know that she won't back off until I tell her.

'Yesterday at Polki Peak-' I start but my Ma shrieks on hearing the name.

'You went to Polki Peak? Alone, in this weather, what were you thinking.' She starts but my Dad urges me to continue.

'I went there because Rosa wanted to go there.' I say and the two of them exchange a look, that tells me they know something.

'I walked into the forests there and suddenly I got entangled and I think the wind spoke up, I am not sure how, and said some words that didn't make sense.' I say stopping to look at them.

When they don't say anything, I continue. 'It said that, "A power looms to take revenge, a voice to misguide the best, an army of soon to be dead, a leader to guide her friends.", that's it then I got released on my own and I ran back home.'

For a while, my parents don't say anything but then my Ma grabs me and locks me in my room.

'Ma open up.' I pound on the door but she just leaves me there, until I give up. It's only late in the night that I hear their voices and realise that they know something has been going on for a really long time.

VI

Six

'Another prophecy, what are the Gods thinking? We were promised...' My mother says, her voice quivering like she is sobbing.

'Urusa, we can't hide her in there forever, plus we don't know if she is really the one, we can be highly mistaken.' My father says but I don't know how my mother reacts because then they close the door of their room, with a huge bang.

Knowing my mother, she would have given my father a glare before making him agree with her on everything that she believed.

I can't believe aunt Yursulana, the lady who never cares, informed my mother. But what more can I expect from a self-proclaimed seer? This is how she predicts the future I think, first, she catches you doing something then informs your parents then tells you "You are going to have dark times ahead, you need to be very very careful" in a strange child-like voice as if she has been possessed.

Of course, you will have a dark time if you are stuck in a bedroom especially when you love the outdoors.

I need to get out of here and go back to Polki, I know now there is something there that will have the answers to what in the world is going on.

Perhaps if Giants are real, probably Rosa is alive too. I never believed in any superstitious stuff, and look now where I have landed, right in the centre of it, the very core of it, where I also believe in the land of dreams to be a mirror of reality.

Science says dreams are our imaginations. A bunch of random information in our brains combined with our fears or desires, but my last dream wasn't even remotely close to what I had imagined it would be when I had started seeing it.

As if you knew you were dreaming until you woke up. A voice replies and I shamefully agree. I hadn't even known then that I was just dreaming.

Who was showing me that dream? Wait a minute, no one can control my dreams except someone who knows powerful magic, and magic is a myth isn't it?

Or is it? The same voice says making me feel a little irritated and at the same time reminding me of things I would usually not pay attention to.

For example, that lamp in aunt Yursulana's van. No, maybe it was a scientific creation that she must have found on one of her quests.

And the Giant? The voice asks me innocently, making me clench my fists. A human with a genetic issue maybe?

Why is my mind asking such tricky questions to my brain? Why am I suddenly so interested in a bunch of mythological crap?

Because you think it will lead you to your best friend.

Aghh why do I have all the answers today? Okay, so step one is, I need to get out of here, but how?

My first thought is the window, but it has a grill around it, and I am not like that Giant who can just break it into two pieces and get out. How else can I get out of here?

The bathroom window? Wait who are you, I am not this smart by myself.

You seriously don't know me? Wait... there is really someone around me that only I can hear?

Not around, but inside you would be more precise. Hehe!

Huh? Who are you, and why are you inside my body, please get out.

See that's the thing, I can't right now because I am a part of you, I am one of your aids.

What? I am definitely going crazy, I suppose. I should just get out of the bathroom window, and take some rest once I reach Polki. All the exhaustion is making me hear things now.

This time there is no added voice in my head and before executing my plan, I write a letter to my parents and leave it on the bed, so that they don't worry as much as they would if they find me missing.

Dear Ma and Papa,
If you find this letter, don't worry and don't start searching for me, because I am leaving to find some answers on my own. I am sixteen now and I can look after myself. If I don't investigate this issue, I will definitely go crazy, I mean I am going crazy already, can you believe there is someone inside my mind now, that keeps answering my questions on its own- on her own I mean- she is telling me that she is a girl. Okay so don't panic, love you, bye, stay safe, please!
Yours,
Selsel

I have no clue why I mention the girl, but what is done is

done now. I carefully climb through the bathroom window and jump down on the cemented floor with a thud. Thankfully the noise is muffled by the routine siren of the officials and I quickly go about my way while being careful of the flashlights of the officers.

It's quite dark now, but it's like my brain has eyes of its own, and in no time I reach the foothill of Polki. Slowly and carefully, I start climbing up, not even caring about the insects and animals that must me roaming around at this time, and in a few minutes I find myself at the top.

As beautiful as plants look in the daylight, they look scary in the middle of the night. I quickly walk past the flowers, the bee from my dream still haunting me and go into the forest. It is just like the last time, dark and damp. At least something is the same. If my dream was completely real, there should be something at the end of the jungle.

Oh, you reached here quite fast, didn't you?

I jump on hearing the voice again, not having expected her to return. She doesn't even care about the shock she's given me and continues.

I was having a nice sleep but the smell of the tree spirits woke me up. They smell so good, don't they? I used to live in such an area once upon a time, how I miss my home, but now I am here, stuck with you, though I must say, I like you SelSel hehe. Now you must hurry, as nice as the tree spirits are during the day, they don't like to be disturbed at night, even by the chosen ones. C'mon, walk faster. Now I am going to sleep again, dreaming about my old home.

The voice quietens suddenly and I let out a breath of relief. How did she get stuck in my mind and what are tree spirits? What did she mean by old home, did she live in a forest too and if so then why is she staying within me now and what about food, how does she get that? I don't feel sick so obviously, she is not feeding off me.

Ugh, the last thought makes me sick and I decide to continue thinking about her later.

Not wanting to experiment with more dangers, I speeden up and in no time, the trees start clearing for real.

Although it is night, lights shine from a distance indicating that there is someone living here for real.

I almost run through the last of the trees and am about to reach the clearing, when an arrow whooshes past me. I get a bit of a deja vu but quickly get back to reality and hide behind the last of the trees.

'Whoever it is, come in the clearing NOW!' A female voice says and I cower more and crouch behind the tree. I mean, death by an arrow is not how I expect to die.

'Did you find it, Gemma?' A voice says and this time I can't help myself. Immediately stepping out of my hiding spot, I get a huge grin on my face before I do something I will regret forever.

'Rosa?' I scream before an arrow hits me on the left shoulder and I collapse but not before seeing my best friend running towards me, worry etched on her face and a girl shouting at Gemma to check before aiming at her targets. I agree, Gemma if I wake up, you and I are going to have some serious talks.

VII
Seven

I find myself back at my house, and this time there is another girl with me. She has green pixie-cut hair and is wearing a pink short dress, the kind of dress that no one wears anymore. It has cuts on the sides and a low back. The dress and the hair would have looked funny on anyone else, I would even say garish, but on her, they look perfect.

She is tall, taller than most girls I have met, not like I have met a lot of them but I know that she is tall.

Despite her height, she is wearing heels and has a small blade in her hand that fits her perfectly. Her baby face makes her look young but there is an air of maturity around her.

'So we are here, but why? Why did you think of this place out of every other place when you had the option to take me to forests, beaches, even a camel ride in the deserts.' She says and right there I know who she is.

'How can I see you now? You said you are within me!' I say, moving back a few steps in shock, stumbling on the sofa chair and falling on it in a weird manner, my head on the seat and legs in the air.

The girl just bursts out laughing, clenching her stomach, even falling to the floor, her hair flying in all directions.

'Ok ok, it wasn't that funny.' I say, but once again as I try to sit up, I slip and find myself in the same position.

She doubles up even more and I can't help but join in. When she realises that I am laughing too, she stops for a second and stares at me in shock but joins in immediately.

Once our laughing fit dies down, she goes and gets me a glass of hot chocolate and some other liquid that I had never seen in the house for herself.

'Where are my parents?' I ask noticing the time. They should have been here by now.

'Well it's your imagination, if you want them to be here, they will be here but otherwise, we can just have a conversation, just me and you.' She replies and although I don't understand what she means by my imagination, I reckon talking to her would be a good idea.

'So, who are you?' I ask sitting on the edge of the chair and taking a long sip of the hot drink that for some reason tastes like air.

'Oh shoot, time for introductions!' She says excitedly, running her hand over her hair and smoothening the non-existent knots before continuing.

'I am Maya sweetie, the princess of nature spirits, a royalty in the courts of mother nature.' She says, her voice full of love and kindness and a little bit dreamy as if she is thinking of her home.

I stare at her in shock. There is no way that she is a nature spirit. Even if she is, why is she sitting here with me in my imagination?

I close my eyes for a second and when I look back, she is still there, sitting elegantly with her legs crossed, her pinkish drink in her hand, the huge smile on her face making her look more like a little girl than a princess and her eyes looking at me in a mix of concern and joy.

'Say something, go ahead, feel free to ask me questions.' She says in a deep, funny voice and I really can't believe her even more.

'You said this is my imagination.' I say to which she frowns and makes a face with her lips going up in one direction and one of her eyes squinting.

'Well yes, but this, you and me, this is real, only the place is imaginary.' She says quickly in a nasly sing-song voice.

'So you are a royalty, then why are you living in my mind?' I ask unable to contain my curiosity.

She gets a pained look on her face before she mutters something inaudible and in a flash, her smile is back.

'Going with the difficult questions first huh? Usually, people want me to do some magic, and grant their wishes but fine. I was cursed because I apparently pranked my mother. I am to stay with the black-headed one who will be one of the finest heroes ever aka you, no pressure, just saying.' She says with a smile and takes another sip of her never-ending drink.

'So if you are princess of nature that means you pranked the queen of nature? How? And you are mistaken surely, I am not a hero in any way!' I shriek, sitting back against the sofa chair's plushy backrest.

'Firstly, it's MOTHER Nature, second, that's a story for another time but she used to love me and she might have forgiven me I think at least, and third I don't make mistakes so stop denying and start accepting. You are a chosen one like the girls you will meet when you open your eyes. You all have great destinies. You will meet some new people, reconcile with some old ones but you will fulfil your FATE! Do you understand? I will try to help you as much as I can, but I am just a protector. I can't fight your battles, just guide you. Tough times are coming and unless you put your doubts aside and start believing in what you see, you are going to make things a hundred times harder than they already are.' She says and I look at her in fear.

As sweet as she looks, she can be real scary when she wants to be.

'Too much sweetie pie?' She says as if she didn't just scold me for no reason. I mean she did have one reason, but she is not thinking from my point of view. She is not in my shoes.

'Look you have a day or two, you can be as confused, surprised, scared whatever you want to be, but your first enemy is already on his way. You killed his son and he is out to take revenge. Now wake up and start preparing. We don't have much time to get you trained.' She says before disappearing into thin air.

My drink disappears too and slowly my home starts slipping away. I distinctly hear voices and a bright light shines somewhere above me. I open my eyes at once but groan at how the brightness hurts my head.

Someone dims the lights and asks me to open my eyes slowly this time. My left shoulder is sore and my head is pounding. Can this day get any worse than it already is?

Once I am fully conscious, I look around at the concerned faces of three girls around me. Rosa looks relieved, the Gemma girl looks afraid while the third girl, the one who I had also seen in my dream, looks- well there are no visible emotions in her posture.

She stands there with her hands crossed as if waiting for me to stand up and go back to where I came from.

'Oh my God, Selina, how are you feeling.' Rosa says, handing me a glass of water that I gulp down in a go. I have never felt so parched in my life.

'I am good now. But Rosa, I thought you were- I searched for you everywhere. Why didn't you tell me? I found your clothes on the hill and then a few days later the fishermen gave me a finger with your ring- I-' I start sobbing, unable to control my emotions on seeing my best friend alive and well. She holds me, no longer trembling like before but like the Rosa she was prior to the punishment.

'I am here Selina, it's going to be alright. If you have been guided here too, it means that you are a part of this team and we are going to be together now.' She says and I am shocked. Rosa didn't even acknowledge the fact that we were best friends, that I had been searching for her for two whole months, she straight up jumped to the fact that only because I reached here on my own we were going to be spending time together.

The old Rosa wasn't like this. She would have told me why she didn't contact me, would have been excited to show me around her new place and even introduced me to her friends but she didn't.

She got up after saying what she had to say and left with the other girl following her, leaving only Gemma with me.

'Look she has been through a lot so yeah.' Gemma says and leaves too after a few minutes of fidgeting and I am left there thinking if I am still dreaming or if this is real.

Yes, this day did get worse than it already was.

VIII
Eight

After having a pity party for about an hour, which involved crying, pacing around the room and changing into a new set of clothes that Gemma had pointed at before leaving, I chug another glass of water before deciding to explore the place.

The minute I move out of the room, I hear a clapping and turn around, but there is no one and that's when I realise what's happening.

'Maya, you are back.' I say in my mind, obviously to not look crazy.

'Of course, I am, it was frustrating to see you cry and have all those sad thoughts but I am happy to see you moving on. Friends are meant to be traitors, it's nothing new. At least she didn't stab you in the back like Brutus.' She says casually with a small laugh and I can't help but wince at her words and think who Brutus is.

Words are indeed mightier than the sword and have more power to hurt you and leave wounds that never fill up.

'Look, I am not sure what your friends did to you but I am sure Rosa has a reason for her behaviour. She isn't like that.' I say unconvinced by my own words. This time Maya lets out a small angry shriek before muttering something like 'breathe' and letting out a small sigh.

'Well, I hope for your sake that whatever you said is true, I wasn't lucky to have decent friends but I pray that you will be.' She says in a gloomy tone and I get a feeling that she is not being honest with her words.

'You don't want me to have friends, isn't it? Wait did you do something?' I ask, the worst of thoughts suddenly surrounding me.

'What, no! It's true that I don't want you to have friends but in no way I am trying to sabotage your friendships, I am classy like that.' She says and purposely takes a long noisy sip of whatever she is drinking.

Wait how is she drinking something inside me, am I like a house for her, but she is taller than me, ok I don't want to know, forget about it.

'So do you know why she is acting like that? I mean you being a princess and all, your servants might have told you something.' I say sheepishly.

'Huh they did, but why should I tell you.' She says haughtily.

'Because you said you are here to help me!' I say in frustration. How can she forget what she told me yesterday?

'Well, that's right too. Look I can't tell you everything that's happening in Rosa's life because that's her story to tell, but right now someone has made her believe that you are going to betray her and-'

'-and so she is not talking to me because self-preservation is better than living with a broken heart.' I complete Maya's sentence and I can imagine her looking at me with sympathy.

'But why couldn't she come and talk to me? Haven't I done enough to prove that I am her loyal friend?' I say not able to wrap it around my head that Rosa doesn't trust me enough to even communicate with me face to face.

'Sometimes insecurities make you do things you don't expect to do. Selina, you are different, you try to find answers but not everyone is like that. Some people- they just try to get rid of the shady parts of life than explore them till the end and emerge as winners. Rosa, she- Gemma was right, Rosa has been through a lot maybe space is what she needs right now.' Maya says before disappearing again but it won't be me if I take people's advice and just leave my friends alone.

If I have arrived here, and if there is indeed a Giant coming to kill me, I am not dying before finding out what's going on at this place, with these girls, with Rosa!

I continue walking angrily in a random direction, hoping to find anyone but all I find is silence.

The place looks like a palace with huge white pillars, swords hanging for display, old, dusty curtains and wide windows that open up to the view of the jungle. How has no one ever reached here?

It has all the feels of an ancient building, I wonder how it survived in the first place.

As I walk through, I suddenly see light coming through from a slightly ajar door and as I walk near it, I also hear some murmurs.

'Are you sure you want to send her away?' The girl from earlier says.

'You heard what the prophecy said Gina, *a trusted friend will lead you to trouble*, she is my trusted friend but I am not interested in falling into any more trouble and suffering for no reason. And trust me when I say that she is trouble, I have seen her rebel first hand.' Rosa says and what I hear shatters me.

After everything that we have been through, I never expected Rosa to be saying this but I guess Maya was right, friends are not meant to be trusted any more worth fighting for.

I pick up a vase kept on a table next to the door and throw it in anger before running back in the direction I came from.

'Selina… wait… please stop.' I hear Rosa and Gemma screaming once they come out and see me running but I don't. I run till I reach a door at the end of the hallway, opposite to the one I was put in and yank it open before running into the forest, thanking my luck for the door being an escape from the melancholy palace.

The girls only follow me till they reach the door and once they are sure that I have run out, shut it with a loud bang making it clear that I am not welcome anymore.

I can't believe what I have just been through. Did they really follow me only to shut the door behind my back? I wasted two months of my life looking for Rosa only to be called Trouble and gleefully get cut out from her life.

I run and run, till I see the flowers again and climb down as quickly as I can despite the evening approaching quickly.

If she doesn't want to be found, so be it. I can't help her anymore.

In my haste and melancholy, I forget to check where I am going and when I land, I find myself in a well-lit area, that's definitely not my village.

Too exhausted to climb back up, I walk into the unknown land, hoping to find shelter. It's the worst decision I make, but I have no other choice.

The maps never mark this place or show it as occupied, I wonder who lives here. The lights shine brightly unlike my village which always has only a streetlamp or two working.

The houses are bigger too and I see a few children playing around the corner. They are dressed like me, in bright colours. Suddenly I am thankful to have landed here, had anyone seen me in this stupid yellow tunic and white pants, I would have been beheaded.

A van passes by and the children yell happily on seeing it. They all receive a few boxes of what I assume is food, and it's only when I see one of them eating from his box that I realise how hungry I am.

I find a place to sit under a lamppost, hoping no one would object to me and continue to look at the children enjoying their day. They look so carefree, so jolly unlike the ones in my village who are not allowed to be too happy.

A while later, they go home and I find myself gazing into nothing but the empty lane, wondering what is this village.

Sometime late at night, when I have nearly dozed off, I hear the sound of another van. It stops in front of a house, and a boy jumps out. The van immediately speeds away after leaving him there and it is then that I see him looking at me.
He is wearing a blue shirt with brown pants and has a bag in his hand. I can't make out his features from so far away but there is something familiar about him.

Suddenly he starts walking towards me and for a moment I want to disappear into thin air but then I see his face and I feel a mix of joy and panic something that is reflected on his face on seeing me closely too.

'Trub?' I manage to say in a whisper before he pulls me along and pushes me inside his house.

IX

Nine

'Selina, What are you doing here?' Trub asks me after he has checked the doors and windows for the hundredth time.

His house is well-furnished and as big as it looks from the outside.

After pushing me inside, he had quickly locked the door and shut down the curtains like he was hiding a criminal. Yes, I am not allowed in this village but that doesn't mean he should panic so much.

But maybe I am overreacting. This is Tooth Village probably and it's known to be a scary place. He has all the right to be afraid. I should be grateful he at least brought me inside.

'I-uh-I went to the Polki Peak and forgot which side I climbed up from.' I say not wanting to lie but not wanting to give away the truth either.

The betrayal of Rosa makes it hard for me to trust a guy I haven't met in years. Trub has not changed much except for the fact that he has grown really tall and has gained a little muscular weight. I wonder what kind of work he does to have such muscles. Tooth Village is famous for black magic but looking at him I don't think he can do any magic at all.

Whenever I had imagined Tooth Village, I had thought of men with long hair and beards and women dressed like my aunt chanting something all day long. I had not imagined a well-lit place with happy children playing on the street or everyone living in well-built houses like Trub's.

The aformentioned boy stares at me with his brown eyes, as if he is looking straight into my soul. His dark hair is messy and a few strands are falling on his forehead. He still has the same sincerity on his face that he had back then with the only difference that instead of a smile he is now looking at me with a frown.

'Has the kingdom sent you to spy on us.' He says after a while and the way he says it somehow reminds me of Rosa's words a few hours back.

'You know I am not like that Trub. I didn't know where I was running in panic.' I say defensively yet my words resonate with honesty, although I know that he won't trust me. I shouldn't feel this way but all I know is I can't trust anyone again. Until he proves his loyalty I won't tell him anything.

'So did Rosa send you here?' He asks and I am shocked. Does he know that Rosa lives there?

On seeing the surprise on my face, he just shakes his head before going into another room, leaving me standing there all alone. Did they all know something was up? Had they all been communicating all this time?

Questions start filling my brain and I can't help but think how much of a fool I have been. To think that these people were my friends. I can't help but reminisce and the more I think of it, the more I realise that I had always been that person of the group whose presence didn't matter.

Swallowing my self-pity and noticing that Trub has still not returned, I quickly move towards the door and run out in the cold night. Not thinking, not feeling, I once again just keep running in a random direction till I pass all the lights and land in the middle of a clear land.

I was so engrossed in moving away from everyone that I didn't even notice my cheeks were wet because of tears and my feet had blisters that were bleeding.

I look around to see the lights shining at a distance from where I am standing. Where exactly am I now?

There a few trees at a distance and the ground is covered in sand. The only source of light is the moon and the scattered stars blink away like little diamonds littering the sky.

I walk a little more and find a tree on one end that looks really safe. When I sit down, I feel my body aching from the exhaustion. Examining my feet, I tear a portion of my tunic, to clean the blood, clenching my teeth due to the pain. What a fool I am! I left everything behind to search for a girl who doesn't care only to run like a sentimental child and meet another friend who doubts me.

The tree opposite me suddenly moves before I feel a huge vibration on the ground. It bends down suddenly to my horror and that's when I realise I have landed in the enemy's house.

'Look what we have here. I thought that I would have to walk some more distance to find you, but you are sitting here on your own, in my territory, ready to be beheaded. Hahaha'

No, no, no, how did this happen? How did I not notice the pop of colour in this blatant darkness?

'Maya you said I have time.' I say in an accusatory voice.

'Well, that I did but you came here on your own so now we don't.' She replies in a matter-of-fact tone and I can't help but close my eyes in panic. The Giant I had seen last time was really a child compared to this one.

This Giant was so tall that even the tallest trees were like little plants in front of him. He was wearing clothes similar to the other giants in my dream and had a huge scar on his face that made him look scarier.

He laughed for a few more minutes, all the while muttering to himself how he couldn't believe his eyes before raising his bone-like weapon and bringing it down with a roar to hit me.

I freeze. Time moves slowly as I see the weapon coming towards me when I feel something pushing me from inside. My upper half moves to the other side before I feel a push to my legs and I find myself rolling funnily. Had this been a comedy, I would have laughed but right now all I feel like is weeping.

The bone misses me by inches but the next hit comes so fast that I find myself being tossed like a ball many yards away.

Pain flares up my back like it is broken and my head spins so fast I find my eyes closing on their own. I distinctly hear Maya's voice asking me to get up but I can't move.

I almost give up when the Giant says,' It will be fun to destroy this village before killing your parents. How the master will reward me for clearing his enemies, hahaha.'

'My son, look how I kill this girl to avenge you!' He says, looking at the sky as if he can see his son there before moving his large branch-like hair from his face and getting ready to strike me again.

Something inside me awakens the minute he mentions Ma and Papa. They are all I have now, and I can't let them die for my mistakes.

Using all my strength I roll immediately when the giant tries to hit me again and keep doing so until I feel the sand to be wet. The wind blows and I hear the sound of water moving. Oh, how the dark camouflages the water and makes it look like land.

The giant smirks as if has me cornered and tries to hit me again but I roll towards him and tickle his dirty feet, making him slip on the sand, in an attempt to kick me away, and fall into the water. A disadvantage of being so tall is that you cover meters to fall into something that isn't even that close.

He screams loudly, thrashing his body to get up, his legs nearly killing me from moving so much when he stills completely.

I expect him to stand up in a second and kill me for tricking him, but he doesn't.

'He died, the water is extremely toxic. You should thank your ancestors for leaving this gift for you.' Maya says sarcastically and I understand her anger. My ancestors didn't exactly try to keep nature safe, and that's why here we are, living like the Stone Age once again. Well not exactly like that but not as comfortably as our ancestors too.

Once my body realises that the battle is over, my back feels broken again and my feet start burning because of the blisters. The Giant's body starts releasing a toxic smell and like a miracle I once again find myself walking away before falling on the ground near the tree where it all started.

My shoulder that had been hit yesterday, once again triggers up, hurting like it's dislocated and I feel broken, mentally and physically.

The last thing I see is the light in the distance before I pass out again, just like yesterday, just like the day I fought the baby Giant; feeling like a murderer bearing the punishment for her crimes.

X

Ten

I am floating in the darkness, a peal of demonic laughter ringing in the background. I see a person in a hood, staring at me from far, face hidden yet blood dripping from what I assume is the mouth.

I feel disgusted, nauseous even. It raises its hands to reveal its face but before I can see it, I am pulled down below. This time I lie under the stars, a soft breeze gently caressing me, making me feel relaxed. I almost close my eyes when I hear my name. Someone keeps calling me but I can't see the person.

'Selina, please wake up. Selina!' The person desperately calls out but sleep tempts me. How long has it been since I have slept peacefully like a child? How long has it been since I have not had to worry about trivial matters or lost friends or Giants coming to kill me? This place feels good, this place feels like home.

'No Selina, you can't sleep here. Please fight the demon that sings you to sleep.' A girl says and the word demon catches me off guard. How can a demon sing me to sleep? Aren't demons ugly with rough loud voices?

I try to lose myself in the feeling again, the feeling of tranquillity and wholeness but the moment is gone.

My mind is on autopilot after hearing the word and now I find myself restless, bracing myself for the attack but it never comes in the way you expect it, isn't it?

A small boy steps out from behind a tree, a flute in his hand, his eyes weeping tears of blood, his hands like skeletons. As he moves closer to me I realise that he is not a little boy but a full grown man.

He places the flute near his lips and before I can hear his music, I feel something wet being poured on me. I scream from being drenched and wake up with a start. When I open my eyes, I find myself in a strange bed.

The lights above are dim, and the place smells like homemade food but to my surprise, I am completely dry.

My old clothes have been replaced with a dark tunic and my back doesn't ache. Even my shoulder seems completely healed. Where am I and how long have I been here?

'Finally, you are awake.' A voice says, a voice I didn't expect to hear so soon.

I get up from the bed and step out of the room, to land in a dim hall with candles lit near the window. On one side lie some things I don't recognise and on the other stands the person I met so briefly last time, the person who owes me some answers.

Before I can utter a word, Maya asks me to put all judgements aside and thank the person for taking care of me for three whole days.

With the kind of injuries I had received, it's hard to believe that I am better so soon, but it is how it is. I am cured, every part of my body is like new now.

'Stop staring at me and have this soup. It's not as good as your mother's but it will energise you.'

'Aunt Yursulana?' I say my voice trembling like I am speaking after ages not three days.

'Yes Selina, now stop acting so surprised. It is indeed me.' She says, rubbing her forehead in irritation. How did she find me? What is she doing here in Tooth Village? I mean her practice is very apt for this place but how did she come here without creating suspicion?

'I- what are you doing here in Tooth Village?' I ask sitting on the chair next to a table, that I suppose is meant for dining but is currently filled with all sorts of plants, vessels and items I don't recognise, and taking the bowl of soup from my aunt's hands.

'You spend treating someone for three days, repairing their broken bones, cleaning their mess and all they ask you is 'what are you doing' instead of thanking you.' She mutters, glaring at me and I feel like an ungrateful child being scolded for misbehaving.

'Thank you, Aunty! Thank you for taking care of me.' I say hurriedly, slightly apologetic for forgetting to say the words earlier.

'Hmm, you are welcome and the question is what are you doing in Tooth village not what am I doing here? I am a witch, I need to come here to collect the necessary ingredients for my spells but what brought you here is what you need to tell me before I send you back home to your extremely infuriated mother.' She says with her arms crossed and I cower in the seat.

'You killed another Giant, I am surprised how you did it without training but you need to beware. Running around aimlessly has helped you against the weaker foolish Giants but it will kill you in a real battle.' She continues before I can say anything, leaving me shocked.

I am starting to realise that my aunt really has some powers like she keeps saying. She is not all bluff, curing me in three days, knowing my whereabouts, she is definitely aware of more things than she lets on.

'It wasn't my aim to kill them.' I say, my voice heavy with emotions, guilt clawing my heart.

'Well, what is done is done and it's better to kill than get killed so don't be so remorseful now.' My aunt says before adding some more soup to my bowl.

'Eat everything quickly then I will help you escape. You can't be seen here. You already made a grave mistake by going with that boy, now just stay with me.' She says and I am not a bit surprised that she knows.

'Can you please tell me one thing?' I ask once I finish the soup and hand the bowl back to my Aunt.

My aunt slowly nods her head, her attention completely focused on me, the bowl shrinking in front of my eyes till it completely disappears, reminding me of the weird lamp from the van.

'Why are my friends not trusting me suddenly?' I ask and this time she is surprised. Out of all the questions, I could have asked her, this one has been the one troubling me the most. I once read in order to succeed you need people who always have your back and if the people I have known for so long have turned their backs on me, how will I ever find friends who will fight the Giants with me in such a short time?

The fact that I have encountered two giants in such a short span of time means more are on the way. I can't fight all on my own and if no one fights, we will all be dead in minutes. I need help and to get help I need people to trust me.

'Everyone has a different destiny, Selina. Not everyone realises it as fast as you have. You are built differently, you are practical not all your friends are. Besides who says you will need them in your first battle? Now common let's go.' She says ushering me out. Her words are similar to Maya's and for the first time, I understand the hint they have been giving me all along.

I am probably going to be facing the Giant army alone and if I succeed, everyone will live but if I die without completing my task, everyone will be gone.

A shiver runs through my spine. How is all this happening? Where did magic appear from again? Where did the Giants arrive from?

'Magic was never gone just muted to keep Earth safe from you devil humans. Now after the Great Climatic Revenge, the cycle has started again. Every monster that was defeated thousands of years back is awakening slowly and an enemy is trying to return. The Giants are just the first step and as long as you train properly, you will be victorious.' Maya says quietly, her voice giving me goosebumps.

As I walk into the night with my Aunt, for the first time I actually notice that she is not walking, she is floating through the air, just a few centimetres above the ground, invisible to an unobservant eye but the events from today have made me vigilant and combined with the fact that my eyesight has improved thanks to her healing, so much so that to my horror, even though she is wearing a long tunic, I see that my aunt doesn't have feet.

XI
Eleven

We walk in silence till my aunt abruptly stops in front of me making me collide with her. We stand there in silence for a few minutes and it's surprising when we hear some hushed whispers and footsteps from a distance after a while, even though the area is dark.

Is someone trying to sneak in without alerting the officials, as my Aunt often does to enter back into our village? How many people are using these secret passages to come to Tooth Village? From the sound, it seems like there is a whole group! Before I can say something, my Aunt turns around and makes a whooshing sound and I find myself standing in the palm of her hand. What did she just do?

'Your little friend alerted the security. I will hide you in my hair, don't make a sound and we shall pass safely.' She says and all I can manage to do is give a small nod before I find myself sitting in my aunt's smelly hair.

I have to grip onto some strands to not fall down as she walks quickly towards the secret passage.

Trub alerted the officials of my presence. What was the point of him acting so secretive when he had ushered me into his house if this was his ultimate motive?

Eventually, I guess, whatever happens, happens for the best. Had I stayed there for too long, I might have been arrested for sure and then the officers here would be having a toss with the Giant to decide who would get to kill me.

Phew, one problem solved...

My aunt stops walking after a few minutes and I hear someone's footsteps.

'Oh Yursulana, you won't happen to have found your niece here, I believe, because if you have, you must hand her over this instant.' A deep male voice says and I crouch down, lying flat on my stomach to hide myself from his eyes. He sounds dangerous and I hope my aunt is a good liar otherwise she would find herself in grave danger because of me.

'Ah Hamilton, you gathered your officers here to question me when just last week you did something you wouldn't want me to tell everyone isn't it.' My aunt says, walking what I assume is a bit closer to this man because of the drop in the volume of her voice.

'How do you know?' The man says, his tone laced with fear as if afraid of getting cuffed by his own men for his crime. What did he even do? Recite a spell he wasn't supposed to or pay a visit to my village in disguise?

'I know everything Hamilton, how many times should I remind you that?' My aunt replies sweetly before walking backwards.

'Let them go.' Hamilton shouts into the quiet night and there is a sound of a door opening. We start walking towards it when the silence is disrupted again.

'You will let her go without asking her where Selina is? You know that we need her.' Trub's voice cuts through the air and I find myself holding onto my aunt's hair even tighter both out of panic and curiosity.

'She doesn't have her boy and the fact is that only you claim to have seen her, so the question is what if you helped her go somewhere Trub? If you wouldn't have been my nephew, I would have sent you for an interrogation, so stop questioning my judgements and use your brain to find your friend. Call Rosa and ask her to inform us immediately if Selina ever goes back to her place.' Hamilton says and I am shocked to realise that he knows so much and yet is so insouciant about sharing the information in my aunt's presence.

Why do they want me now? Last time I met Rosa she had called me Trouble and now she is ready to help Trub and his uncle in finding me.

After the conversation is over and silence descends once again in the area, my Aunt quickly resumes walking through the door without once turning around and soon we find ourselves in an underground tunnel.

It's dark and I can hear a few mice squeak now and then but my Aunt walks through like she knows the place from the back of her hand. Despite the darkness, we never once bang into the wall and I am in awe because clumsy folks like me cannot even think of crossing a place like this with all its turns and twists.

After an hour of walking, we end up at a crossroad and I can only know what it is because of the dim lights that look like artificial flames at the centre of both entrances.

My Aunt quickly starts walking through the left door and for some reason, I get a feeling that we are on the wrong track. My worries go away once I see the village lights shining at a distance.

A cool breeze blows in from the forests and we continue walking in silence. I am about to ask my Aunt something when two officers pop out of nowhere and try to grab my Aunt. I almost save myself from falling by holding onto my Aunt's hair, infact accidentally so tightly that she winces in pain. I am thankful for her not screaming but at the same time, I am left wondering how these officials got to knew.

I can smell a rat named Hamilton even from the distance. No wonder he spoke so openly, he knew all along. Now what?

'Yursulana Stardrew, you are being arrested for crimes you are well aware of. Give in without struggle and we may ask the elders to reduce your punishments.' One of the officers says and the bluff in his voice could have been detected even by a child.

He has no intention of letting my Aunt suffer less. He is the type of guy who will never even help an innocent.

'Landart Tibert, you of all people should be aware of what will happen once I start speaking in front of the elders. You as an officer should know that-' My aunt starts saying when the officer with this weird name cuts her off suddenly with a laugh.

'Yursulana, you have some guts to say this when you should know what can happen to a lone woman blocked by two strong officers.' His statement makes his friend laugh out too when my Aunt does something that makes them stop abruptly.

Their clothes burst into flames and when they try screaming from the pain, their mouths clamp tightly making them suffer in silence.

'Do not ever try to threaten me, you buffoon!' My Aunt says angrily before extinguishing the flames and also curing the officers' wounds because when they fall to the ground they leave sighs of relief.

'You are truly a witch! Fine, you can go, but remember, now you have too many enemies Yursulana, too many enemies.' Landart says and we once again walk out unhurt. Why is everyone up so late today?

I can only hope now that we reach my house safely. We walk for a distance but right before the turn to enter into the village, my aunt makes a sharp left and hurriedly starts walking into the dense forests. I have no option but to hold on tight. It is only when we reach into such dark parts where I can't make out a tree from a clear space, does my aunt pull me out and bring me back to my size.

'From here on you are on your own. Maya will guide you to your parents and instructor.' My aunt says surprising me. Is she really leaving me here alone, here out of all places?

'But aunty, where are you going? You can't leave me here, you heard the officials.' I say desperately, not wanting her to leave me here alone to go somewhere where the officials can hunt her down and even kill her if she is not careful.

'Selina, I don't like people worrying about me and regarding enemies, I have had them for more than a hundred years and yet I have survived pretty well. Remember you are not alone, you have Maya, you have your parents, you will have your instructor and when the time comes even me but for now it's only you atleast in person. Find your team carefully and don't let my efforts today go in vain.'

With this, my aunt lightly touches my hand before leaving me in a strange area with no idea of my destination and no possible way in sight but only one thought lingering in my mind, my aunt is a hundred years old?

XII

Twelve

I walk through the darkness, aware of every leaf breaking under my boots, feeling grateful for the breeze providing some relief in the hot, humid night. Maya hums and grunts every few minutes like she is going through something painful but I have no idea how to wake her up.

How do you politely ask someone who is residing somewhere inside you, maybe right next to your soul to stop dreaming? I try calling her name in my mind a few times but all she does is give a light hum that is no different from the one she is giving out every few minutes.

The forests around our village have no dangerous wild animals but they are full of poisonous snakes so I keep my ears wide open for any sound of slithering.

As I keep walking in a straight path, the Sun slowly starts rising and for the first time, I realise the importance of Sunlight. We take things so casually that we don't realise their importance till we really need them.

The light not only illuminates my path but makes me stop and double-take at the scene around me. There are tall trees with huge green-orangish leaves and scattered white flowers all around forming a canopy over the meadow-like region.

Purple-pink flowers are peaking from behind a few grasses and the whole place looks like a fairytale. If only I had wings and I could fly around!

'Who said you don't?' Huh? Maya is back then.

'Good morning Maya, not a good sleep last night?' I ask purposely to know what she was so terrified of all the time.

'Hmm, memories of the past reminding me to work harder with you my friend! Now that I have been shown the reason for my exile again, the scars I had received ache like fresh and motivate me to train you faster.' She says with a distant voice and I feel a little sad for prying. But isn't it time for her to tell me though, what exactly had happened to her and how she had gotten stuck with me?

Most of the time Maya is just sleeping, singing or nowhere to be found. I can literally count the number of times she has spoken to me but every time she does, it's all about training or battle.

How did I land up in this spot? Why was I chosen to fight the incoming Giant party? Will I ever get the answer or before anyone explains things to me, I will get killed?

My stomach grumbles from hunger and I crave for my mom's food.

'Hungry already? You had so much soup when we started.' Maya says sarcastically, sipping on something as if she is teasing me.

I don't know how I can always know when she is eating or drinking. It's just strange like I can see a small vision of her hand holding onto a glass and a faint outline of her face speaking to me like she is right in front of me but not.

'Before you start commenting, let me remind you that you don't particularly starve yourself the whole day Maya!

You are always eating so you are no one to tell me what to do.' I humph angrily and she giggles to infuriate me further.

'Well, I am happy to see that you have some spark left after all that panicking and sobbing you have done the past few days, Selina. This is life, you have to think of ways to get things. You are hungry, well you are in a forest, it's not that difficult to find food, look around you there are so many fruits. But remember, you will have to work a little to find which ones are edible and which ones will kill you in a shot.' Maya says before taking another sip and humming a strange tune.

As I look for the right fruit, the lyrics to her song make me feel like I have transcended into a different time.

Little roses littering my garden,
Rosy apples for breakfast,
Take a pony to the lake to see the fishes swim past!
One day at a time in the meadows of my kingdom
You see how beautiful my home is
One day at a time in the meadows of my kingdom
You see how life should be lived!
Blue skies spreading away like a blanket,
Birds chirping their sweet melodies,
Take a boat to the island and sprawl under the sunlight forget about your melancholy!
One day at a time in the meadows of my kingdom
You see how beautiful my home is
One day at a time in the meadows of my kingdom
You see how life should be lived!
Grass softer than a pillow,
Spirits beautiful inside out,
Love and generosity drifting like breeze, their magic making everyone beam!
One day at a time in the meadows of my kingdom

You see how beautiful my home is
One day at a time in the meadows of my kingdom
You see how life should be lived!

Maya continues humming the same song again and again and again but it doesn't irk me, instead I find myself humming along with her. Finally, I find myself standing in front of a small pink fruit that looks enticing.

It is shaped like a strawberry but I am sure it is not one. Instead of having a rough texture on the outside, it looks quite soft like pulp. The fragrance is sweet and tempting as well but before I can pluck it, Maya stops singing and literally screams at me to stop.

'Are you out of your mind, I feel deaf!' I scream back.

'Seriously, I just saved you from dying a sweet painless death!' She yells at me while I stand there confused.

'You really don't know this fruit? Butanip, does the name ring a bell now or do you still want to eat it?' She says and all the stories I had heard of as a child come rushing back to me.

Butanip: the most dangerous poison in the world. The kingdom often used it to eliminate its enemies. It's the easiest and yet the hardest way to kill someone. Easy once it's been given to the victim but hardest when it comes to transport. To pluck the plant, one needs to wear special clothing covering all the parts of the body. Even a drop can kill you on the spot.

I move back to a safe distance and take a deep breath. How did I forget the first principle of finding edible plants? Never trust the beautiful fruits- beauty kills.

'That fruit there on your left, the huge one with thorns and a bright yellow colour, that's edible. And yeah a thank you would suffice before you start thinking of the jewels you can gift me for preventing your untimely death.' Maya says in a bored voice that makes me feel like hitting her but okay yeah, I should thank her because of how active she is today.

'Thank you, Maya, your majesty!' I say sarcastically and walk towards the plant, groaning in pain because Maya decides to kick my chest at that moment. How she even does this transition between being solid and gas I really don't understand.

'Stop hitting me please!' I scream before carefully plucking the fruit and peeling it. It looks disgusting but what other option do I have?

Quickly taking a bite, I swallow it before the taste worsens from chewing more. It is a mix between bitter and sour and I have to control my insides from churning and throwing the nutrition away. After taking two more bites with great difficulty, I throw the remaining portion and decide to resume my journey. Little bees I hadn't seen before, swarm on my leftover fruit as if they were waiting for me to finish and I run away from the scene before I become their next meal.

As I run through the forest, I pass a lake I hadn't seen before and it's not long before I find myself nearing a few huts with smoke coming out of the chimneys at a distance.

There are three huts in total and two caravans. Would my parents really be here and who would be my instructor?

I stand for a few minutes while the birds chirp and the leaves sway, closing my eyes to prepare myself for whatever is planned next in my journey.

XIII

Thirteen

Controlling my emotions that are running high like an untamed horse, I start walking towards the huts. As they get closer, I realise they are not as small as they looked from far. With every step, Maya's voice gets lower as if she is afraid, she won't be welcome if other people discover her. How would anyone even hear her, no one can even see her except me though aunt Yuruslana knew about her so my mother know as well, a small part of my mind thinks.

A sweet smell drifts through the air and my stomach grumbles again. I am pretty sure I would eat even the foods I dislike after experiencing that disgusting fruit!

Once I reach the little nomadic civilisation, I take a few moments to look around. There is nothing extraordinary except the huts and the caravans. At first glance, the huts look like they are made of straws but on a closer look, I am shocked to see that they are made of bricks and mortar.

No one is in sight and I can't even hear any voices that indicate someone is here. Taking a deep breath, I walk towards the house closest to me and knock at the door.

A minute passes then two and after almost ten minutes, I find myself standing in the same spot as before. Huffing in irritation, I go and knock at the second house but the same thing repeats!

Where is everyone? Certain that I would find everyone in the third house, I go and bang at the door in frustration. Last time my aunt had called my mother so quickly to complain but this time she couldn't even let her know that I would be arriving in a few hours.

I bang a few more times at the last door, but no one opens up. My frustration starts turning into anger and I almost give up when I remember I haven't looked inside the caravans.

The first caravan as expected is empty with only a few boxes inside that have everything but food. I groan a little from exertion and hunger and slowly walk towards the second caravan that is parked near the first house I knocked on.

How did I not follow the smell earlier? Standing near the door of the second caravan, my stomach makes a loud excited noise from the wonderful smell. A smile breaks through my face as I raise my hand to open the door but before I can make a move, the door suddenly opens on its own, slamming me back and making me fall flat on the ground.

'Here you are. We have been waiting for so long. Now are you going to stare at me from there or get up and get inside?'

I stare at my Ma in surprise as she goes back inside. What is she wearing? Where did she get such colourful clothes from?

Getting up slowly, holding my throbbing nose, I go inside to find my father sitting inside with another man who is dressed in a way I have never seen anyone except Maya dressed.

He has pink-purple closely trimmed hair and is wearing a long blue coat with white flowers all over. His pants are a bright yellow colour and I don't know why he thought they would match his coat. Lastly, he is wearing bright pink boots making him look like a pop of colour in my dark dull world.

My father is also wearing a white shirt with brown pants while my mother is wearing a green tunic and white trousers.

The caravan looks like a rebel camp. No one would be able to guess from the outside that it's so spacious inside. There are sofas on one end where my father and the man are sitting and on the other end, there is a dining table and a kitchen-like area.

'Are you going to continue staring or will you go and wash up and then have lunch? I have prepared your favourite strawberry cake for dessert.' My Ma says suddenly and I quickly go where she points to clean up.

The bathroom is big with a tub in the corner. I do my business and change into the clothes kept near the basin.

The pink tunic is similar to what my mother is wearing and at the same time reminds me of the clothes given to me by Rosa's friend. A sad cloud hovers over me when I remember her but I quickly push it away and after combing my hair into a pleat, and once again washing my hands, go out and sit on a chair near the dining table.

As my mother brings out the various dishes and sets them on the table in front of me, I notice my father and the man talking in hushed whispers.

Maya is still unreachable and I don't even know why I try to say Hi to her.

I pull my plate closer as soon as my mother fills it up with all the things she has made and I can't help but moan at how good everything smells.

Taking a bite of Rice with some Kidney Bean gravy, I close my eyes at the wonderful taste. I know now that I will not always get quality food and it makes me appreciate everything even more.

Stuffing my mouth with a few more spoonfuls of the combination, I move on to the snacks that my mom has prepared and don't stop eating them till I feel like I would burst. I save the cake for the end and every bite is worth the wait. Finally, after I have inhaled the amount of food that I would usually eat three times, I clean my hands and face with a wet hand towel that my mom gives me and look around with drooping eyes.

What can I say, food makes me sleepy.

When I get up to clear the plates, my Ma quietly asks me to go and sit near my father. When I get closer the two men quickly stop talking act look at me.

'Hi Selina, I am Jackson, your instructor.' The man gets up and extends his hand in my direction.

When I touch his hand to return his greeting, I nearly flinch at how cold it is.

'Maya?' He says, the minute he feels my hand and I am surprised at how he would know about Maya.

An electricity buzzes inside me until I feel something leaving my body and that's when I see Maya standing next to me in full glory.

Today she is dressed in a golden shimmery long dress with slits on the side and her hair is long and red. She has a slight blush on her cheeks which I don't understand but the way she looks at Jackson I can tell she knows him. I mean she has never revealed herself before, not that anyone has realised her presence before except aunt Yursulana.

Before I can say anything, I notice that my father is frozen in his seat, his mouth slightly open as if he is about to say something, I turn around to see my mother is frozen as well, one of her feet slightly raised like she was about to move when the time stopped.

I look back at Jackson and Maya who are still staring at each other, neither saying a word.

'Um guys, how did you stop time?' I ask confused.

'How did you not get affected?' Jackson asks as if just realising that I am present.

'Why did you think I chose her not her friends.' Maya replies proudly.

'Of course! Look you are not supposed to be here, it's not safe.' Jackson says and his words affect Maya so deeply that she takes a step back with her head hung in what I assume is a disappointment.

'Why did I expect any different behaviour from you?' Maya says her voice heavy with emotions before taking a deep breath and continuing in a normal voice.

'I am not going anywhere, if you are so scared, I will train her alone.' She says, crossing her hands but before Jackson can say anything she snaps her fingers and goes and sits on the chair.

My parents looked around in a daze until they understood what had happened.

'Maya, never do that again, you get that?' My mother screams before giving me a half hug to Maya.

My mother knows Maya. How?

'Yes, we have known each other since ancient times. We were best friends until we were separated by that devil of her mother. Something about witches and nature spirits not being friends.' My mother says casually.

'You are a witch too?' I ask in shock.

'Of course, and your dad is a nature spirit that is why you are special. Why else do you think you were chosen as the first warrior?' My mother says and it makes sense. But I don't have any powers or magic, why was I chosen?

'Why was I chosen, how did you know I was going to be chosen, or the Giants are coming back?' I ask but before I can get answers my Ma shushes me.

'We will tell you everything but first, let everyone have lunch. While we finish, you go and have a nap. You are going to have a long day today!' She says and I have no option but to follow her to a room in the first house and settle down with a queasy feeling.

XIV

Fourteen

As I lie there on the humongous bed, in a strange white room bare of any other furniture or wall hangings, my gut tells me to get up and check on everyone in the caravan.

Although my mother was persistent about me staying here, something in her voice felt off, what if some danger is on the way and she is trying to protect me by hiding me here? She has always been like that, her first reaction is always locking me up to save me from problems unbeknownst to me.

Tossing the comfy white blanket aside, I run towards the door but as expected it doesn't open. I check the windows but they are jammed too! So my instinct was right all this while, something is happening outside that my mother doesn't want me to be a part of.

Disappointed for blindly falling into Ma's trap, I sit on the bed and think about everything that's happened so far. It's so hard to digest the fact that up until last month, all I was worried about was finding my friend and now here I am, two dead Giants, meeting a friend I didn't think I would meet so soon and realising everyone in the family is magical, later.

I shouldn't be so calm about all the secrets but surprisingly I am. All my life I didn't second guess anything that was told to me but now I even distrust fruits!

I don't know how many minutes pass with me just sitting and staring at the wall in front of me but the more I look at it, the more I can see the buzzing lines that make the wall look like an illusion.

Getting up, I touch the wall and lo and behold, my hand passes right through it. Next, I put my leg through the wall, and they go through too.

The next second, I find myself running through the wall and back into the open space in front of the house. Woah, that was easy!

Tip-toeing towards the caravan, I am surprised to find the door open and loud voices booming out.

'Maya I am not going to leave you here. You are coming back with me and then I will return to train Selina.'

'You've got to be kidding me! You left me a century ago, you chose to serve my mother rather than trust me, you stood there while everyone mocked me and called me a fool and today when my findings are proving to be true, you once again want to get all the recognition and leave me on the side to be berated by the spirit community, don't you? Guess what, unless you kill me in a dual, I am not going anywhere with you!'

I stand there paralysed like a fool, the silent sobs of Maya slicing through my ears like knives. I won't let this guy take her away. She is my friend, the only person who was there with me through these weird dark days of my life.

Suddenly as I stand there, thinking of what should be done, my mother comes out and glares at me.

'How did you come out?' She says with her hands on her hips, her face devoid of any emotions.

'Through the wall, now move aside, Maya needs my help.' I say pushing past her before turning around to find her standing there in shock.

'And next time you try to lock me up-' I start saying before realising who I am talking to and silently turning away, but anyway, she needs to stop doing this, it's irritating.

I spot Maya sitting on one of the sofas, her shoulders trembling slightly and the man responsible for her pain standing with his head hung low on her side. My father is nowhere to be spotted and something tells me he must have left the minute this conversation started.

'Maya, are you okay?' I ask, staring down at the Jackson guy. He is almost a foot taller than me so it should technically be staring up but who cares?

'Selina! How... I should have known by now though that you would see through it. How long have you been here?' Maya says, her voice slightly quivering before she puts on her happy mask again.

'Enough to hear that this man has hurt you in the past and decide that I don't want to be trained by him.' I say and the man smiles to my shock. Why is he smiling like that?

'I am glad to see that someone is here to take care of my Maya.' He says, leaving me speechless and Maya infuriated.

'I am not your Maya, you lost the right the day you left. You are here to train Selina, just focus on that, besides you have been replaced in my life. I don't need you!' She screams and I see Jackson's aura dimming at her words.

Before he can say anything else she takes my hand and leads me outside.

'I am sorry for all the drama, your father has gone to make sure the barriers are up and talk to the tree spirits to hear any updates. Come on it's time for me to teach you some basics of magic.' Maya says as we walk towards the first caravan.

'What is your story, Maya, please tell me what is going on, why me?' I say, not wanting to do anything else before knowing the truth.

She lets out a long sigh before leading me to a log of wood behind the first house. It's inconsiderate of me to ask her to relive everything especially after she just had a breakdown but I only realise it once we are seated on the log and Maya is about to begin.

'Look Maya, I am sorry for pressuring you, you are already not yourself today-' I begin before she cuts me off.

'I was wondering where this humane part of you is, but it didn't take long for it to show, didn't it? Don't worry, I won't break so easily. Let's begin now. Don't interrupt me before I finish.' She says and I nod excitedly like a little child, making her laugh.

'This story is of a century ago. As I told you earlier, magic has always been around, just not visible enough for you humans to realise and misuse it for your greed. I was born almost at the same time Earth became habitable. I saw the Dinosaurs, I saw all kinds of monsters, I saw all epics like the Ramayana and I also saw humans running so fast towards modernisation that in the blink of an eye, my world was dying.'

'My mother wasn't happy and therefore the whole Great Climatic Revenge happened a century and a half back. I was never in its favour but who was I to go against it? I was always pampered and spoilt by my mother, how could I speak up against her? Then fifty years later, I was going around making sure all the wards were intact, gloating for being given the work that only top warriors were given, but at the same time being despised by everyone in the kingdom because they believed that I was only chosen because my mother was-is the Queen.'

'Then one day I found an entire section of the ward at the intersection of Hell and Earth broken and warned my mother but by the time she arrived with the forces, it was intact like before. No one can mend broken wards except my mother and her ministry and so my mother got angry. She assumed that I had been trying to get her attention by lying about something so cardinal. She warned me to not make a fool of our family in future and left but I was hurt. I wanted to prove to her that I wasn't lying but every proof that I found went missing right before she could see it with her eyes. She doesn't believe in photographs, only her own eyes. I could see the demonic activities starting, the Giants waking up one by one and being under the control of a Dark One but how could I make her see the things I was seeing? The last straw was when I told her about a Giant and it pretended to be a friendly one in front of her. That day I was ousted from the kingdom. Everyone laughed at me while I packed my things and moved out.'

'Your aunt found me, she was the first person who believed me. Your father was also an outcast for marrying your mother so something clicked between all of us. We all became the best of friends. Then one day, your mother had a vision. Visions are messages from God, a sort of a glimpse into the future. She was told that you would be the first warrior. The slayer of everything wrong and that we would be training you, that I would be your protector, and just like that my life changed. I hid for a while till you grew up but now I am back because you need me. I can't tell you everything right now, but now you know more than most and that should be enough for you.'

When Maya finishes, I feel sympathy for her. I just hold her hand and we sit there lost in our thoughts for a while.

'What about Jackson and did your mother never try to reach out to you after that?' I ask unable to control my curiosity. Maya lets out a small laugh at my question before looking away.

'My mother doesn't talk to the ones she kicks out and Jackson, he was my husband till he decided to agree that I am shallow.' She says and leaves me sitting there feeling awful for asking her the last question.

XV
Fifteen

'Are you going to spend your entire time sitting here, or are you going to start with your training now? The Giants are starting their journey tomorrow, we don't have much time.' I look up to see Jackson towering over me after a few minutes of sitting alone in guilt.

'I am definitely not taking your help, you can't be trusted.' I say getting up to leave. If he can leave his wife alone after so many centuries, how can I trust him to be on our side if the spirits switch sides or something?

'Whatever I did was for Maya's sake and I don't think a young girl like yourself would understand it, but I am here now and either you can use my help or I will anyways be leaving tomorrow for a few days and then I don't know if I will be able to help you at all.' He says with a sigh and I feel furious.

He just arrived and is leaving again without apologising to Maya, how can he be this way? Instead of staying back and learning from him, I decide to leave. He will be gone tomorrow, he can't obviously teach me anything in an evening.

I start walking away when I see Maya returning and gesturing for me to stop. I turn around to find Jackson standing in the same spot as before, looking at Maya with hope but she doesn't spare him a glance.

'You need his help, he is the best in the field. If you want to save the world, stop running and start learning.

My problems aren't yours to deal with, he is your teacher, respect him and start your training.' She says with her hands crossed before going to sit back on the log.

I let out a frustrated scream before raising my hands in surrender. Why is everyone so confusing these days?

'Fine, let's train!' I scream before I am struck from nowhere and I find myself fallen on the ground face first.

The first rule of war is, always have your guard up, even when you are sleeping. The enemy is not going to wait for you to take position before starting the fight. One distraction and you are going to be hanging dead.' Jackson says extending his hand in front of my face to help me up but I know better now, so I get up on my own.

'I can see that you are a fast learner.' Jackson says once I stand back up, with a huge toothy grin that makes him look like a young boy before kicking me out of nowhere and making me fall back into my initial position.

Groaning I get up again and before he can say anything punch him right in the face. I would have boasted my plan in satisfaction a few years down the line had he not held my hand tightly before it could hit him and twisted it back painfully.

'Rule number two: analyse your enemy's weakness before blindly attacking and dying a brutal death. Giants are huge and one flick of their thumb can also throw you miles away, always remember that.' He says before gently leaving my hand which is red from pain.

'Why are the Giants coming back anyway? Do they have a motive other than killing us?' I ask trying to ignore the ache in my arms and shoulder and standing up tall.

'Well, they have been rotting in hell for ages. If someone gives you your favourite things for doing their homework, you would do it, isn't it? Someone very dark is trying to return but first he needs to get all the powerful forces on his side to defeat the Gods. The Giants are his first weapons for doing exactly that. They are strong but foolish, always have been that way, and dying to take revenge for being kept in hell for so long. They can easily make the weaker spirits turncoats once they arrive other than killing the most useless entities, i.e. humans, a win-win for both the parties.' Jackson says and before he can hit me again I move two steps back making him smile in appreciation.

'So who is this dark person? And can't we use guns to kill these giants' I ask before trying to hit Jackson again, but once more he easily deflects my attack and in the process also pushes me hard on the floor.

'First, guns are ineffective on anyone except humans, they feel like a tickle honestly. Second, the dark person is someone very powerful, someone who was once loved by all but someone who misused his gifts and thought he was better than the Gods and was therefore defeated and imprisoned in the most high security but dangerous part of hell. He has slowly been gaining power now, piece by piece and we need to end his weapons if we want to end him.' Jackson says as I get up again, feeling a little dizzy from all the pushing and kicking.

'Can't we convince the Giants to be on our side?' I ask, I know it's a stupid question but I need to find a way to distract Jackson if I want to hit him for hurting me so many times in a row.

'Well, would you switch sides to help the elders of your community, knowing how much they mistreat everyone? No, right, that's Giants for you, they are in your shoes and they would definitely work with anyone but the elders who would put them in hell again.' Jackson says laughing at my stupidity and I seize the opportunity to move as discreetly as possible and kick him to the ground.

For a moment everything stills but then Maya starts clapping and that's when I know that I have indeed managed to attack and hurt the powerful Jackson.

Jackson gets up and claps too with a smile on his face and I genuinely feel a little happy for the first time in almost three months. The emotion feels strange but it fills me with a warmth that had been missing for long.

'Good, very good, that's exactly how you do it, Selina. I understand now why Maya stays with you all the time. You have potential. Once we unlock your magical capabilities you will be able to do wonders but I can see that it will take some time. For now, let's focus on your strengths. Start running around our setup.' Jackson says before whistling and I look at him in confusion.

'What are you waiting for girl? Run, now!' Jackson yells and I start running immediately.

At first, I feel nothing. I mean I am just running around the houses and the caravan, how hard is that but within half an hour, I find myself sweating and panting, however, Jackson shows no signs of asking me to stop.

He sits there on the log, right next to Maya whispering something continuously, trying to get her attention which he never gets because she is busy singing a very bad version of a new song that she heard somewhere. I mean it's new for me but she seems to know the lyrics really well.

Although I appreciate the meaning behind the song and know it's meant to encourage me but the way Maya sings it, makes me want to stuff my ears with cotton, it's really that bad. It's a surprise how Jackson is sitting right next to her without even batting his eyelashes. Maybe he is using magic to block her voice.

I keep running, refusing to give up until my legs start shivering uncontrollably and my head starts spinning. I try to run one last round but my legs give up and I fall down, unable to move or speak.

'Oh my God, Selina, I am sorry, I completely forgot to ask you to stop.' Jackson says crouching down next to me as I try to gather enough energy to scream at him. How can he just forget something so important?

Maya fulfils my wish, when she sees me finally after her song ends, by punching Jackson and asking him to get lost before helping me go to a room in the third house and lie down.

'I am sorry, I didn't notice sooner Selina. Go to sleep now, tomorrow we will practice something better and easier.' She says before turning off the lights with a snap of her fingers and leaving me alone in the darkness.

Will I really be able to save the world, but how?

XVI

Sixteen

I don't sleep a wink the entire night. My body is sore and my mind is restless. Who is this dark soul that is trying to stir so much trouble? Jackson said that the Giants need to be stopped, that they need to be killed again but how will that work if there is a gateway now from Hell?

I toss the blanket aside and walk out of the room barefoot to find Maya sprawled on a sofa in the hall. She has a glass of whatever liquid she keeps drinking always clenched tightly in her hands and her eyes are closed as if she is sleeping.

'Can't sleep Selina?' She says, making me jump in fright and she just laughs in response, her eyes still closed. How is she able to see with her eyes closed?

'I have a doubt. Something that Jackson said is not making any sense to me.' I say and she just hums.

'Are you even listening?'I ask a bit worried about her behaviour. She has not been herself ever since Jackson's arrival. I mean she used to ignore me before too but it was complete silence, not a small half-hearted hum.

'Jackson said that I need to end the Giants but if they are coming back from Hell, won't they return even if I kill them?' I ask partly curious to see her reaction and partly desperate to see her be normal again.

'Hell is a huge place, Selina. The part they were caged in has been unlocked now and Yam is not able to find the keys to lock them again but when you kill them again, Yam will be ready to capture their remnants and lock them in a new place. He is a one-man army you know- Yam- he needs help sometimes.' Maya replies taking a sip of the bright blue drink.

Whatever she says makes sense but is still unsettling. What if someone steals the keys again and unless the new chambers are safeguarded immediately, all these so-called weapons come out again anytime.

'Do you think someone is helping this Dark One? He can't possibly be doing this alone if he is not completely free.' I ask and Maya opens her eyes and looks at me with a proud smile.

'Strange isn't it that a young girl can make all the correct speculations but the folks who have been around for ages are still trying to pretend as if everything is fine! Yes, there is a traitor but the traitor will only be revealed when the time comes. The Giants will reach soon and they will start their attack from the Greog village. We need to teach you everything and travel there soon. If we don't stop them before Hutata, they will use the minor spirits to energise the dark one.' She says and goosebumps run down my spine.

The fear of failure is stronger than before and the thought of seeing my loved ones getting killed makes me feel nauseous. I need to learn everything quickly!

'I am awake, you are up too, shall we start?' I ask but Maya just lays back down again to my surprise.

'Just lie down for some more time. We are just a few miles from Thornos, unless you want to get spotted by some overly suspicious elder, we need to wait for the horn to indicate they have gone back.' She says and my eyes go wide in astonishment.

'Well, won't they spot our houses and caravans? Why are we in this area?' I ask in a hushed voice, afraid that if I speak too loudly, we would be caught.

'That's magic for you, they can't see us as long as we are inside, though some of them have been around for too long to not smell it even from a distance.' She says taking another sip of her drink, her stance completely relaxed as if it's not a big deal.

'Are you not afraid of them finding us here, they will never believe us if we tell them about the Giants.' I ask not able to digest the fact that we are cooped up near a dark prison.

'What makes you think that they don't know about it already? The King, the elders and some of the King's close associates know the truth. How do you think your kingdom survived when the rest of the world died?' Maya says and a light bulbs in my head. I had never thought of people being present in other parts of the world but now that Maya has mentioned them I feel bad for surviving when they didn't. Technically my parents survived but still.

'So they won't mind us preparing for the war here?' I ask.

'Now, I didn't say that too. Many of them are corrupt and have spread a false hope amongst the others that the Giants will be friendly.' She says, closing her eyes again.

'Why are you ladies up so early? You disturbed my beauty sleep.' I turn to find Jackson standing there in a pair of baby blue pants and a half-open maroon robe, his hair tousled from sleeping and eyes only half open.

'How long have you been eavesdropping? Still finding clues to convince my mother that I am and will be a traitor.' Maya says before I can say anything and even I wince from how mean she sounds.

'Maya, we have been over this-' Jackson starts saying but before he can complete his sentence Maya snaps her fingers and disappears somewhere.

'Great! We were supposed to start training, where did she go?' I say in a whiny, disappointed voice. Why did Jackson have to do whatever he did? Why can't these men have an ounce of brain and sentiments?

'Why did you leave her alone? And don't tell me it was to protect her blah-blah-blah. I want the real answer because I can't see her like that and unless we resolve the issues between the two of you, we won't be making any progress with team building. You and I both know that it's only a few of us against don't know how many Giants and if we are not united, we are not going to make progress.' I say with my hands crossed and Jackson gives out a long sigh before rubbing his eyes.

'You do know that it's only you against them right? I don't owe you any explanations. Maya knows the reason-' Jackson starts saying but I cut him off angrily.

'Oh right and it's so wonderful that she can't bear looking at you. Tell me the truth NOW because I know that you must have lied to Maya.' I say and Jackson slightly pulls his hair before going and sprawling on the same sofa Maya was lying on a few minutes back.

'I had no choice! Her mother, she threatened me with Maya's life, she wanted to really punish Maya because that's how she is. Her emotions have no limit, if she is angry she is monstrous and if she is loving she will feed you from the palm of her hand. She said that she will kill our child, she-'

Jackson cries before realising that he has spoken too much and then just like Maya he disappears.

Maya and Jackson have a child? How have I never met this child then? Why does Maya never talk about her child? I can't believe how a grandmother can threaten to kill her own grandchild but the thought is painful.

I can only pray that the child is safe and happy. I wish Maya and Jackson resolve their issues, they are both clearly in pain and unhappy with how their life is going. Once this Giants drama is over I can help them to rescue the baby from Mother Nature, assuming she is the kidnapper, and hoping that I survive that long.

I never thought that the elders would be in the loop with things that I once believed were a lie. They always act so self-righteous that I could have never dreamed that they would be in peace with spirits and Gods.

A horn blows off at a distance a few minutes later indicating that they have left Thornos but before I can go out, my mother enters in panic.

'Your dad has been captured by the elders and charged with treason!'

XVII

Seventeen

I can't believe my ears, Ma has to be kidding. Why would they capture my father? Do they know why we are here?

'Selina just stay here while I try to get your father out. Under no circumstances leave this house, do you understand me?' My Ma says before rushing out the same way she came in.

How can I stay here while those elders hurt my father? As I make up my mind to go out, the room starts turning dark little by little. For a layman, there are no apparent changes, but I have always been observant when it comes to light. What is happening?

A few seconds pass by and the room slowly and steadily grows darker, almost dark enough to look like it's dusk.

'Maya? Jackson? Guys, please stop playing with the lights!' I scream but there is no response apart from the shaking of the vase kept on the table in front of the sofa. There is something wrong here, I turn around to run but the door vanishes out of sight.

A shrieking sound echoes through the house, making me wince at how painful it is to my ears before smoke starts filling in. Is something burning? I turn around again to check but I get my heart in my mouth when I see the same little man I had seen in my dream standing there with his flute. His eyes are no longer bleeding but he looks haunting.

His skeleton hands are covered in patches of different shades of skin and his face has multiple cuts making me feel dizzy with fear. Despite his ghastly appearance, his smirk is as visible as the moon on a clear night.

'Selina!' He speaks barely opening his mouth, even the bare effect making more blood drip from his face.

His voice cuts my ears like glass and all I wish is to run away but I have no clue how. His presence makes me feel like falling to the floor and crying reminding me of every wrong that I have done, reminding me of how I killed the two Giants, how much of a sinner I am, but I stand there like a soldier, every minute making me feel weaker, every second like I am drowning in toxic water.

'How will you save the kingdom from my friends when you couldn't save your father from mere humans? Quit now or you shall suffer, everyone you love will dieeeeeeee! Hahahahahaha.' I fall to the floor in pain, the weight of his words crushing me like a mountain before I feel like I am burning all over. My ears hurt from listening to his voice and I smell smoke.

Before I can reply to him, the darkness vanishes suddenly and is replaced by light. I close my eyes from how bright everything appears before I feel someone's hand on my shoulder. I jerk in panic to stop the devil from touching me but to no avail. I can't believe how much of a fool I am. I should have run the minute I saw the changes happening but no I stood here observing like a nincompoop. Now I will die at his hands before I can even learn how to save the world.

'Selina.' A soft feminine voice says that I distinctly recognise as Maya's but how can it be her when just a few minutes back I was facing the Bleeding Man? Is he making me delusional now, am I already dead and imagining things one last time before I am sent to Hell?

'Selina, please get up, you are scaring me.' Maya's voice says and I feel a hand shaking me. What if the Little Man is impersonating Maya and wants to kill me with his eyes?

'She saw him.' Now I am hearing Jackson's voice too. Listening to his voice makes me a little hopeful that it's really Maya and Jackson, but how can I trust my ears? The Little Man could be faking both voices, he looked capable of it.

The Little Man had a painful voice, the rational part of me says but my mind refuses to believe it. I lie there for a few minutes, cowering on the floor, shivering from remembering the things the Little Man made me believe were my fault. He was right, I can't save the world. I-

Cold water splashes on me out of nowhere making me jump up and nearly head-butting Maya. What had happened to me and how did it stop as suddenly as it had happened? I no longer feel as depressed and guilt-ridden as I felt a few minutes back, instead, I find myself burning with anger.

How dare he step into a house my family built and play mind games with me? The next time he appears I will show him who the real boss is!

'So you met him.' Maya says in a grave voice when I finally look up at her after a minute. Water drips down from my hair and the clothes cling to me like second skin but I am not as bothered as I should have been.

All I care about is how terrible I was in front of the enemy.

'I know you are being hard on yourself right now but you were excellent. Many minor spirits have surrendered to him out of fear despite being so much more powerful than you, and he wasn't even in his current form then, you were brave and you can't expect yourself to stand tall in front of him without any knowledge of magic Selina.' She says when I don't say anything. How does she know how I am feeling?

'You said that the Giants would help him to get minor spirits on his end, how is he doing it alone?' I ask confused. Is the traitor so powerful, that the dark one is already getting better each day, Giants or no Giants?

'I was wrong in underestimating the Giants. We need to go to Greog once I give you the basic training in magic and find out a way to end the power source they are using to make the dark one more powerful. Meanwhile, Jackson has left to gather information from our allies.' She says clenching her fists.

'Wasn't Jackson supposed to leave later today?' I ask, wondering what made him leave so quickly, did my questions agitate him?

'He was, I have no idea why he suddenly wants to help us more by gathering information but someone is keeping an eye on him for me, don't worry.' She says turning around and I can't help but feel that she is hiding something very important from me.

'What about my father? My mother said that the elders have arrested him, we need to go check.' I say moving towards my room to change out of the wet clothing before I catch a cold.

'It was a prank.' Maya says, stopping me in my tracks. A prank? Why would someone play a prank on such a serious issue?

'What do you mean?' I say turning around, unable to believe that someone would dare to joke about the elders arresting my father.

'Rosa wanted information about you, so she decided to lie to your mother about your father's arrest. She thought that your mother would give away your location but your mother is smart. She is on the way home now with your father and yeah you might feel happy to hear that she taught Rosa a lesson today she would never forget.' Maya says with a smile and though I can't help but smile back, I also feel a pang in my heart that Rosa of all would joke about the elders.

No one knows better than her how cruel the elders are. She experienced their torment first-hand and yet she tried to prank mother. My mother is fiercely protective of our family so I know that Rosa will never try to play with her emotions again but what I can't believe is that Rosa also revealed herself to my mother. Did she come down from the Polki Peak to reveal her true intentions?

'Also let me tell you that Rosa has returned to the village now with her two other friends and the elders are hiding some secret about her from the rest of the tribe. There are rumours about her friends' origin and the tribe is not very happy.' Maya says and I wonder how she gets so much information all the time without her spies revealing themselves.

'Did you not get to know when the Bleeding Man invaded our house?' I ask but Maya just looks away instead of answering.

'I am sorry Selina, I couldn't come to save you when you needed my protection, I was trapped too.' She says after a few minutes and it's only the flush of her cheeks that makes me feel that she is telling the truth.

XVIII

Eighteen

'How did that devil come inside, I don't understand?' My Ma asks for the hundredth time in an hour. The minute she had returned with my father, one look at our faces and she had realised something had gone wrong. We had decided to not tell her about anything but how do you lie to someone who already senses the problems from miles away?

Apparently, the area around the houses and caravans was under some kind of spell to keep everyone away. The fact that the Bleeding Man could still enter inside was a huge deal. It meant that either one of us was a traitor or he was already powerful enough to do anything that he pleased. The later thought was terrifying since it meant that we didn't have much time or power to stop him and it meant that we would all be dying too soon.

Amongst all the conversations and questions I was also starting to realise that Maya had been exceptionally quiet about her disappearance. Did she have something to do with this new problem that we encountered today?

Every time we tried to discuss her absence or Jackson's sudden decision to help us, she brought up something that completely changed the course of the topic and diverted our minds from the fact that the Little Devil's appearance today had something to do with her or Jackson.

'Ma please stop pacing around, I am feeling dizzy by looking at you.' I say in a barely audible voice, afraid of telling my mother anything in such a tense scenario. I brace myself for a good scolding but I am surprised when I see my mother actually sitting down with a sigh.

'Maya, can I ask you something?' We all look at my father in disbelief on hearing his voice. My father is a man of a few words. He mostly just keeps to himself but he is extremely dedicated to the family. Whenever you need a solution, he is the man, but I have never once seen him starting or even taking part in a conversation so it's surprising to me. It's weird for my mother too who stares at him with wide eyes.

'Yes, Kirst.' Maya says in a tired voice, a part of me says that she is going to disappear any moment but another says that she is going to fall asleep.

'Maya, truth is what acts as an adhesive for a team. If there are lies and deceptions, you end up losing no matter how much of a strong strategy you have. I am not much of a diplomat so forgive me if it comes out rude, but I can see that you are hiding something. I understand that we all need privacy at times but this is about my daughter's safety and I won't take it lightly. I request you to tell us the truth at once.' My father says and my Ma and I literally look at him with our jaws hanging open. It's hard to believe that my father said so many words at once.

'Kirst listen-' Maya starts saying but my mother cuts her off.

'No you listen, Maya, we have known each other for years and I have never once questioned your decisions but

Kirst is right today. If we have distrust, this alliance won't work. I know that it may seem that we are pressuring you but it's about my daughter-'

'And what about my daughter Urusa?' Maya bursts out and we all look at her in shock. Did Jackson tell Maya something or was Maya trying to keep her child out of this situation all this while?

'You have a daughter?' My mother says, her voice heavy with emotions. Emotions that mostly reflect sadness. It must be strange to know someone for so long and yet be unaware of something so crucial about their life.

Maya looks down in guilt, her eyes tearing up and her face convoluted, not revealing what she is exactly feeling. Why did she never tell anyone about her child?

'Listen, I think we have had enough drama for a night, I should leave-'

' Maya you will leave when I tell you to. What is going on? You need to tell us the truth. If you have changed your alliances because of your child, you need to tell us now!' My Ma literally screams and I feel confused by all the emotions running in the room.

On one hand, I want to give Maya space but on the other, I don't want her to leave like this. Clearly, she is conflicted and needs help that she is refusing to take. If she needs help to rescue her daughter or something, I will be the first person to offer help, but our team is lacking communication. The older members not telling me half the things is one thing but them having communication gaps is even more dangerous!

'You can't make me talk Urusa and yes I have changed my alliances so now it's just you, your crazy sister and your husband who need to save your clan. Goodbye!' Maya says and disappears into thin air before I can say a word.

Ma bursts out crying and father rushes to console her while I just stand there like a fool. She had told me that I didn't need friends, that I would be alone and yet I had trusted her when she had said that she was my protector, that we were a team.

The truth is that everyone who pretends to be my friend leaves and I need to put it in my head that I have to fight my battles alone. If the Giants are coming here to end our tribe, it is because I killed two of them without a shred of remorse, and so I need to protect everyone from their anger, alone.

Quietly leaving my parents in their melancholy, I leave the house without a second thought and start walking in the opposite direction of where I had come from towards Greog. If the Giants are on their way, it won't take them much time to reach Greog and considering their size, they will kill everyone without any effort.

As I walk through the forest, I can't help but think how I would stop them. Maya went away without teaching me any kind of magic and I am not even a trained fighter. How will I win with only the knowledge of a few tricks for dodging the enemy?

My stomach grumbles but I don't stop walking until I hear the howls from the dungeons of Thornos and stop in my tracks. What exactly is going on there? Has the prison been attacked by wolves?

Sweat drips from my face both from walking so far in a day and fear. The howls and grunts increase as minutes pass with me just standing there paralysed. I need to see what's inside but I can't digress from my aim. If I get delayed, the Giants will reach, but if there are wolves, I also need to help the tribe shoo them away.

I feel like I am back at the crossroads in the cave. As I try to arrive at a decision, I hear movement in the leaves behind me. I quickly turn back, ready to disarm the enemy but I am shocked when I see Gemma step out from behind a tree, her arms bleeding, her face looking like it has been clawed at before collapsing near me.

Who hurt her like that? Did she brave the wolves alone or did someone attack her with a sword? Not feeling like leaving her alone with her wounds, I collect some leaves from the trees near me and dress her wounds as best as possible with them.

Of course, water is essential to clean up but I use the little moisture in the leaves as efficiently as I can to clean the blood. Then I cover each gash with a leaf to protect it from insects and sunlight and tie up a piece of her shirt that is tearing away on its own, tightly on the biggest gash on her hand to stop the bleeding.

I then drag her in the open to where the elders can see her while making their way back to the village and quickly run towards Gionia before I am spotted and questioned. I can only pray that Gemma survives to tell her story to the tribe.

XIX

Nineteen

Walking in Gionia is like taking a stroll in a shady, dark lane where you feel like you can be attacked at any time. There is no trace of light and as I move through, I completely lose track of time.

The strange part is that the area is dead quiet. How can a forest be this still? There should at least be the sound of wind playing with the leaves or even animals moving but there is nothing and it makes the place scarier.

The temperature is also cooler than the village which is like magic because there is no indication of what is causing the drop. I take every step like it's my last, my heart racing from anxiety and fear. What is this place?

My stomach grumbles loudly multiple times and my muscles ache. My mind drifts through a hundred different scenarios and I can smell danger. Every logical cell in my body tells me to turn back and run.

What kind of forest has a long straight path with trees only on the borders like decoration? But I keep moving ahead till my legs give out and I fall on the floor to find it wet.

Is it water? Is there a stream flowing through the forest, but then why didn't I feel it before? As I raise my hand up to smell the liquid, I suddenly see something flash through between two trees at a distance.

Curious, I immediately get up using all my strength and start moving towards it. I hardly take three steps when someone jumps on me.

I fall on the ground, hitting my head in the process and feeling crushed by the weight of whatever is holding me down by my neck. I try to fight back, kicking it with all my might and even trying to claw at it with my teeth but it doesn't work.

My head starts feeling heavy from the hit on the ground and my eyes start drooping on their own from the oxygen cut off. I start giving up slowly and accepting my death when someone comes out of thin air and knocks out the person choking me.

As I lay there gasping for air, I hear the noise of the two strangers fighting until there is a huge bellowing sound and the air grows thick with the stench of blood.

I do not dare to think of who might have won but when the victor comes and gently picks me up, I am slightly relieved to know that I am not going to be killed, at least immediately.

We move in silence. I have a hundred questions but I don't know how to ask them. Who is this person?

Why did they help me? How did they get to know that I had been attacked?

The person holds me up tightly and I feel like a baby cradled up in her parent's arms. The entire way to wherever I am being taken to is similar to the path I had come from. I want to walk on my own but my body refuses to be strong. I also feel embarrassed by how my stomach grumbles every few minutes.

'You are really hungry aren't you?' The stranger asks me after a while and I am stunned by how deep and nice his voice sounds after hearing practically nothing for such a long time. He has a different accent that I can't place where I have heard earlier.

'Yeah.' I reply in a barely audible voice. Speaking even this small word hurts my throat like hell and I groan in pain.

He doesn't ask me anything else after this and we continue walking for an indefinite time. I fall asleep after a while. My dreams are haunted by the Bleeding Man who keeps telling me that I will die and Maya who keeps reminding me that I will not have anyone by my side. I also see glimpses of my parents looking at me in disappointment and the tribe members accusing me of failing them. The voices keep growing louder until I feel someone shaking me awake.

'Are you alright?' The stranger asks me and I feel guilty for what I call is dreaming out loud. I can feel him sitting on my left, his face turned towards me and yet masked by the shadows. Who is he and what was he doing here?

'I am sorry for troubling you, just saw some bad dreams!' I say in a whisper, my throat still hurting from being choked.

'Don't worry, this place is like Hell, it just feeds on your fears till you either go crazy or die. It's best to stay awake. The good thing is we don't need to travel much now. Will you be able to walk on your own now?'

He says and I am terrified. Had he not been here, I would have definitely died in my sleep. I also feel bad for making him carry me so far.

'I can walk now and thank you for saving me.' I say, not knowing how else to show him my gratitude for saving me twice.

'Alright so let's continue before another creature finds us, we don't have much time.' He says and helps me get up.

We walk side by side, with him holding my hand as if afraid I would try to run and get stuck again with another monster attack. There is no conversation and for some reason, I feel it's because the creatures would then be able to attack us faster by tracking our noise.

Why do these creatures stay confined in this forest and how does he know about them so well? I didn't even get a good look at what the one that had attacked me had looked like but its strength was far greater than anything I have ever faced before, not that I have faced a lot of enemies, but having so much strength is scary especially when you are not even that big.

We soon arrive at the last edges of the forest, the clearing visible just a few steps ahead and it's only then that I start feeling normal. At first, everything seems a little blur, with my eyes adjusting back to the light but then it feels like a boost of confidence to be back in my type of area.

I immediately look at the stranger, to see who it is that helped me and when our eyes meet everything stills.

He is not as surprised to see me as I am to see him. He has that look on his face that says, I came to help you knowingly but how would he have known of my location? How did he get involved in this war?

'Slice, is it really you?' I ask unable to believe the fact that he is here. He looks different, just like Trub did though I know for sure that he is taller than Trub and more muscular. He also has a light beard and the only reason I recognise him is his eyes. He has heterochromatic eyes, one is blue while the other is greyish green. He is the only person I have ever met who has such beautiful eyes.

'Selina, yes it's me! I can't believe you have grown so much.' He says before giving me a hug and I can't believe how different it feels to meet him after meeting Trub. I had always thought that Slice didn't consider me much of a friend, he only kept up with me because of Rosa, but whatever I had believed for so many years is proving false with time. How bad am I at judging people?

'What are you doing here? How did you know Gionia so well and how did you know I will be there?' I ask all in one breath before groaning in pain from how saying it hurts my throat.

'I will answer all your questions but first, we need to reach our base at Greog before night falls and we lead the monsters to our safe place.' He says and we start moving again, my mind full of questions with one of them standing out the most.

'Should I trust Slice?'

Twenty

We walk through the trees and stop right before a fence around the huts. The huts are colourful and small. They look temporary but strong enough to withstand the harsh weather I have heard Greog has.

I take another step forward thinking we are going to climb through the fencing but Slice holds my hand and makes me stop. He looks around a few times before raising his hands in the air and creating a dense fog around us. We walk through the fog and right before we touch the fence, Slice once again closes his eyes in concentration. That's when the fence moves apart revealing a completely different place than I had seen earlier.

There are tall buildings in the village, taller than the ones that I have ever seen, with atleast ten floors. The few people I see walking are dressed like the ones in Tooth Village and it makes me question if it's only our tribe that dresses in the darkest way. How did I never know that all the villages except ours are living in such luxury?

'Are you going to continue staring with your mouth agape or are you going to follow me now?' Slice says breaking my chain of thoughts and I turn to look at him smiling.

'Why are you smiling?' I ask smiling unknowingly after a long time. The last time I smiled was when I had defeated Jackson and I must say stretching my facial muscles again today, feels good.

Jackson's memory also reminds me of Maya and I find my grin slowly disappearing. What if Maya's words were true and I am supposed to lead this battle alone? Should I risk getting too friendly with Slice in such a scenario? All my other friends left me one by one, if Slice does that too, I will die from emotional damage before the Giants even come after me.

'What are you thinking Selina?' Slice asks me with a frown and I just shake my head in a no, unable to formulate the right words to say what's on my mind.

'You know, it was brave of you to come here alone. Jackson had informed me that you had started out on your own and I was a little unsure in the beginning if you would even survive Gionia for ten minutes, but you did and I am proud.' He says after a while of just staring at my face and I feel betrayed.

He has been working with Jackson and Maya? They said they won't support us anymore. And what does he mean by 'he was unsure of my capabilities'? Do I appear to be so weak and foolish? But I am foolish, aren't I? I started out with an aim and found myself right in the trap of my enemy. I turn around to walk away and hide the pain coursing through my heart but Slice holds my hand again.

Why does he keep doing that? Why does he keep holding my hand to stop me? Why couldn't he have just let me die in the forest? Why go through the pain of saving me?

'Why are you walking away Selina? Why did my words hurt you? The old Selina would have put me straight for questioning her strength and willpower but where is she now?' Slice says and I clamp my mouth shut to prevent the outburst that's ready to flow out like a river.

My eyes get blurry with tears and I get goosebumps all over. He is right. What has happened to me? Why I am getting so emotional over people?

Taking a deep breath, I look up at him with as much ferocity as I can muster and instead of frowning again at my expression he smiles, a huge toothy grin to be exact.

'Now you feel like you again. Come on, we don't have much time, the Giants are on their way and we need to discuss the strategy to defeat them with our army.' He says and we start walking towards a big white building that looks like a pole because of how thin and round it is.

'Slice, do you not know that Jackson and Maya have switched sides?' I ask and he just keeps walking like I did not say a word. We pass a few people on the way who greet him with excitement and even give me a welcoming nod.

'Jackson has always been on our side. As for Maya, you never know whose side she is on until the end. Her child is in trouble right now, so she has sided with Asura, the minute her child is safe, she will be back, asking for forgiveness.' He says after a while, leaving me confused.

'Is Asura the Bleeding Man? And how do you know so much about Maya and Jackson?' I ask curious to know how everyone at this point is aware of the terminologies and nature spirits except me.

'The Bleeding Man? Nice name!' Slice says laughing out loud.

'Almost makes him seem like an easy target than a dangerous monster. Yes, by the way, his name is Asura.

Coming to Maya and Jackson, I have known Jackson for a long time now, because he is my mentor. I know Maya only because she is his wife who always falls into trouble for siding with the wrong people at the wrong time. Jackson spends a lot of time cleaning up her mess.' He says and his portrayal of Jackson is completely different from that of Maya's.

'Maya said that-'

'What? That she was right about spotting the opening but wrongfully punished? The truth is she did spot the opening but she also tried to close it herself first, with a wrong spell I might add, which led to it opening further. Jackson spotted her mistake and immediately called Mother Nature, who closed the doors but it was too late by then. Maya has always been careless and despite multiple warnings, she had been flouting the magical norms for a long time which led to her getting banned from the courts. Jackson tried to save her from this punishment but she pushed him away. He still tries you know, but she never gets tired of playing the victim. At this point, he only bothers because of their child.' Slice says and I am shocked.

Is he telling the truth? Is Maya really such a good actress that she fooled my parents and my aunt for such a long time?

'Do you know their child?' I ask but Slice just looks forward. I look in the direction he is looking at to see a tall man coming our way. He is dressed like a warrior in black pants and a matching black shirt and is carrying a spear. His hair is closely cropped and he has a tattoo on his neck.

He has the aura of a powerful man and from the way that other people walk behind him, it seems like he is the leader. Next to him, walks a woman almost half his size with golden-brown hair and a beautiful gentle face. She looks like his exact opposite in a blue tunic but still has an aura that commands respect.

Slice gently puts his hand around my shoulder and looks at me with a warning gaze. What is he trying to say? Are these people our enemies? Should I not look at them anymore?

'Slice, nice to see that you are back with this young friend of yours. Selina isn't it? Slice begged us to let him risk his life to save you because he feels that you are the one, I hope you will be worth the effort.' The man says in a commanding tone and I can't help but look down while giving a subtle nod.

Once he goes away, I look at Slice with a questioning gaze but he just pulls me along till we reach a wooden door. He taps it thrice to reveal a set of stairs going all the way to the top. We climb three floors to reach a corridor with multiple doors and it's only then that Slice turns and looks at me again.

'This is our floor. You will be staying in my room and I will be teaching you everything I feel you should know before the war. The man we just met is the head of this village. His name is George and the woman was his wife, Greogina. They are sweet people but at the moment they don't trust anyone. You can sleep for a while, once I come back we will start.' He says, before leading me inside a huge room that has a double bed, a table, two wardrobes and a door that I assume leads to the washroom.

He gives me a black shirt and a grey pants to change into before leaving me alone, wondering how I have once again landed in a strange zone and if my parents and aunt will be arriving here soon as well.

XXI
Twenty One

'How long have you been here and the main question is how did you reach here?' I ask Slice once he returns back to take me for training.

'There is so much you don't know Selina and it's best if I tell you my sob story after we defeat the Giants but a summary version is that once I started realising that I was different, I started feeling detached to the mundane things and wanted to learn more about magic. My father could not accept the fact that his son was a chosen one and exiled me from the palace. The whole affair was kept a secret and thus the kingdom does not know that it doesn't have a crown prince anymore. But moving on, I fell into a lot of trouble for a whole of two months and that's when Jackson showed up to help me. He taught me how to use my powers and brought me here to Greog where the people immediately took me as one of their own.' Slice says and I can't help but feel bad at what he's gone through.

My mother might scold me at times but one thing I know for sure is that she will never leave me alone. I wonder how she might have reacted to seeing me missing. I shouldn't have wandered off without letting her know but what else could I have done? She would have locked me again if I had told her about coming to Greog alone.

'How did you meet Trub?' Slice asks me once locks the door and starts leading me in the opposite direction of where we had arrived from.

'I was depressed after meeting Rosa and in a hurry, I climbed down from the wrong side of Polki. Somehow I ended up in the extended section of Tooth and that's where I met Trub, more like he spotted me sitting under a pole. Then he took me to his house and I felt he was up to no good so I left. I saw him again when I was returning back, he wanted his uncle to catch me but they failed.' I say. There is no use in lying to Slice when I feel that he already knows the truth.

'I am sorry for Rosa and Trub's behaviour. They have to fight their own battle and they are really stressed about it but it is not an excuse for how they have treated you. I hope you will forgive them in future.' He says but his words just make the wounds deeper.

They had all been in contact with each other, they all trusted each other to share their secrets and had the fates not selected me to fight the Giants, they would have never looked me in the face again. They need me so one of them is trying to pacify me and get my help but what if I fail, then what? Will they go back to trying to sacrifice me or will they stand by my side? The chances of the latter are next to null so this means either I will die or I will die. Great!

We reach the end of the corridor where there is a huge door marked with an 'X'. Slice looks at me with an odd expression before pushing the door open and entering inside. Although I was expecting to enter a garden of some sort, there is nothing even remotely close to my imagination.

There is a big hall, with bare blue walls and no windows. When Slice had mentioned training, I had expected weapons and open spaces not a closed blue hall with nothing! He walks inside and I half expect him to conjure a different place like earlier but he just sits down and looks at me like he wants me to do the same.

I sit next to him, looking around to check if something changes but except for the door shutting and getting locked on its own, nothing happens. I look at Slice who is sitting with his legs crossed and eyes closed and has a calm around him, and copy the posture but I am left waiting for the positive vibes.

All I see when I close my eyes is death and destruction and the Bleeding man standing right in the middle of it all, smirking at me, challenging me to stop it.

As I open my eyes, I find myself in a different place. Gone are the blue walls, instead I find myself amidst a garden. The flowers are different from those at Polki and the breeze is hotter. I walk around calling Slice but there is no trace of him. Where did he go?

I try to search for the huge door to step out but find nothing. Tired, I am about to sit under a tree when I spot a butterfly. It's nothing like I have ever seen before with its rainbow-like colour and intricate patterns and it feels like it's trying to tell me something.

Subconsciously I start walking towards it. It's like I am hypnotised by its beauty. As if sensing my presence it starts flying towards a black flower that was previously hidden from my eyes.

Should I follow it? Last time the bee in my dream hadn't been gentle, in fact, it had burnt everything in its way. If we look at nature, bees have always been dangerous but butterflies are beautiful. I look at the butterfly which is fluttering its winds rapidly as if indicating its impatience.

One step at a time, I start walking behind it, keeping my ears and eyes on the lookout for trouble. How did Slice escape from this place? The flowers are soon left far behind and we have entered a bright forest. Is it Gionia? But how can it be? Gionia was dark and gloomy whereas this is so bright that it literally hurts my eyes.

We stop in front of a cave and the butterfly turns towards me once as if making sure I am really there, before entering inside. It wouldn't be the best idea to go into an unknown place that I have no idea of, isn't it? As I contemplate, I feel something wiggling around my feet. I look down and to my horror, a dark green vine is wrapping itself around my legs. I try to get out of its hold but as hard as I pull, the vine holds on tighter, almost cutting through my pants and bruising my legs.

What the heck butterfly? You were also evil weren't you? The vine slowly moves upwards, wrapping my body like a gift and it almost reaches my abdomen when I hear a laugh. A deep throaty chuckle that sounds like something I have heard before. Before I can recall the voice, a woman steps out. She is tall, taller than Maya too with long hair tied in braids and a huge hammer in hand. She is dressed in a short skirt that looks like a huge red blanket tied together with another huge black blanket that is tied with a blue blanket and an animal skin one-shoulder blouse.

Now I know where I had heard the voice. Baby Giant's voice sounded similar to her laugh. Don't tell me she is his mother who has come to avenge the father and the child.

'So you are the one who is going to end my family! You tiny girl! Hahaha, how foolish are the Gods, you still have time, run before I single-handedly end you, poor baby.

Hahahaha!' She says before she starts blurring and completely disappears and I find myself back in the blue hall.

Slice is sweating next to me and looks like is in the middle of a bad dream. Before I can wake him up, his eyes open on their own and he looks at me in terror before masking his expressions.

'So did you see our first target?' He says after a few seconds of regaining his calm. What does he mean by the first target? Did he have some role in my vision?

'How and aren't the Giants going to attack together?' I ask, why would they go one by one?

'They would never attack together. This is an opportunity for them to show their present king, who is the most worthy of becoming the next ruler. They will attack one by one but their attack strategies will be different as all of them have a different power. Tell me, now what you saw in your vision?' He says and I don't like how he yet again presses on his initial question. Will he tell me what his dream was about?

'I don't like being forced Slice. If you share your dream, I will share mine too!' I say and he frowns.

'Selina, what I saw is not important but what you saw is, so now tell me.' He says, his voice simmering with anger and irritation.

How can I tell him when he won't share his findings with me? Is this a trap? Lock me in a magical room that shows you dream messages from your enemies and then declare me an enemy too.

'Fine, keep it a secret but know that not all secrets are worthy of other people's lives.' He says before leaving me alone and once again the room blurs until I find myself sitting at the same spot as before only this time with Slice looking at me in panic.

'Are you alright? It's not like the room to show someone so many messages at once. Let's go back and rest for the day, alright!' He says before helping me up and taking me outside the room. I feel a bit dizzy and lean onto him until I pass out completely.

XXII
Twenty Two

I wake up with my head hurting on the sides. My body hurts too like I have been in a battle and my eyes sting when I try to open them. Someone dims the lights and I can't see anything but a silhouette that I assume is Slice's.

'Slice?' I say my voice coming out broken and almost like a whisper.

'Selina, oh my God, you scared me to death.' He says running towards me and giving me a hug that feels like he is crushing me even when I know he is being gentle.

'What happened?' I ask once he sits next to me after adjusting the pillows to help me sit up and setting the lights to a level that feels good to my eyes.

'You were attacked in your dream. I should have never taken you there without making sure that you were protected with the charms.' He says in a serious tone.

'Attacked?' I ask confused. I don't remember being attacked, I don't even remember most of my dream somehow except for the fact that I had seen a lady Giant who looked like- like - I can't remember. How do I not remember? I can recall every dream that I have ever seen but how do I not remember this one?

'Don't worry. You are okay now! You won't remember the attack but I can assure you it was a brutal one. Dream Giants are known to attack in such cowardly manners. I should have been more alert. You could have died for God's sake!' He says, his voice tearing up.

'Dream Giants? By any chance do they even steal the dreams?' I ask even though I am logical enough to know they do. I just want to know more about them and I don't know how else to continue the conversation since no one will tell me things openly.

'Don't worry, I will take care of them from now on. We don't have to stress about your lost dream, if it was a message from the fates it will be redelivered to you when we go to the message room next time.' He says and I find myself getting infuriated.

Why are they all so deceitful with me? They take all the information but give me none. I am just a weapon I suppose, an inanimate object that want to use to their benefit and discard later.

My fears were true after all. A part of me is scared that I would break down but I surprise myself when I don't. The old me wants to scream out and say that she is back, that she won't fall into this sweet talk and fake gestures again but I don't let her.

Let them think that I am weak and broken, the 'oh so shattered Selina who lost all her friends', they will never know what happened when I bask in the glory of victory.

I have never lost and I never will, friends or no friends! If I am meant to kill Giants then I will and then when this is all over, I will go far far away where they will never be able to use me again.

'Selina, are you alright?' Slice asks in a concerned voice that I can see right through and playing the part of a damsel in distress I just shake my head yes. He falls right into my trap and helps me lie back down before leaving the room to get some food.

Once I am sure of the fact that he has left, I quickly get out of bed and fighting through the pain in my head, get out of the room. Since he might have put some magic to keep an eye on me, I walk out like I don't know where I am going, until I reach the stairs. Racing down through them I come to a halt when I see Greogina standing in front of me.

She looks angry and I can literally see the steam coming out of her ears.

'I knew that you wouldn't help us, that you would run at the first opportunity but they wouldn't listen to me.' She says her voice simmering like a flame that's going to char your bones.

Two guards step in front of me with cuffs but to my horror and surprise, she sends them away. Once they are out of the way she pulls me to a room and I hear gasps. I guess this is the end then?

We enter a huge room that is so magnanimous that it looks like a house in itself. She gently pushes away the curtains on one end of the room and pulls me inside a smaller room that was initially hidden from view. When I turn back I am surprised to see myself being hit by her with a whip, screaming in pain, bleeding profusely but when I look down at myself I am completely fine, not even a scratch.

I look at her to see her smiling genuinely and it leaves me even more perplexed.

'What is going on here, are you trying to present a different reality to your people? Are you not on our side?' I ask standing defensively although I am not sure how I will defend myself against her.

'I care a lot for my people Selina and that's why I don't agree with hiding things from you. Trust me when I say that my husband and Slice will sacrifice themselves for you but will it be worth it when all they have to do is tell you the truth? Look, I will fall into trouble as well when my husband gets to know that I am giving this to you' - She says giving me a small bracelet-

'But this needs to be done. You are going to be our hero but you can't win unless you know why you are fighting. Wear this bracelet when you are alone and know your truth, Selina. Your mother will be here tomorrow, so you might want to know things before that. We need to step out now, they are coming. Don't be surprised when you see yourself bleeding and this is the time to test your acting skills.' She says and we walk back to the place where I had seen her hitting my image. We walk there until the delusion goes away and indeed she is standing in front of me with a whip.

Before she can raise her whip, the door opens with a bang and Slice comes running inside. One look at me and he is trembling with anger and I don't know what I should think as the reason. Is he genuinely angry as a friend or he is furious because he thinks I am his tool?

George comes too and he looks disappointed in his wife. His face is contorted like he knows the truth, like he knows I have the bracelet, courtesy of his wife but he doesn't say anything.

Slice helps me stand up and looks at Greogina pointedly. She raises her hands and hoola-hoo-hoo the blood is gone and my skin feels cleaner than ever before. Once I am back to normal, he gives an angry bow, that I feel could have led him into trouble in other scenarios, before picking me up and leading me out of the room.

I protest but he doesn't listen. Thankfully Greogina's magic also healed my headache otherwise I am sure he would have gotten a whack from me for carrying me like a sack full of tomatoes.

He doesn't stop and we get weird looks from the people around till we reach his room where he just throws me on the bed like a rug.

'Are you out of your mind? You would have died had I not arrived. Are you so eager to end your life, do you not value it at all? Why were you running with your other injuries? I told you in very clear words that I would be back with food. You just don't listen-' He rants while pacing around the room and I know then that I should listen to Greogina and trust him to be a loyal friend.

To irritate him further, I pretend to be asleep but to my surprise, he not just stops speaking but also flicks his thumb across my cheek twice before leaving the room.

XXIII
Twenty Three

The minute Slice leaves the room, I sit up straight and examine the bracelet in my hand. It has round diamonds encrusted along the belt and a red flower-shaped ruby that sparkles brightly in the middle.

To say it's beautiful would be an understatement. I carefully place it on my hand before latching the buckle onto the hook and waiting for a few seconds for the magic to start. Time ticks but nothing happens. I even close my eyes to meditate away into the story that is supposed to be my truth but except for nearly dozing off a couple of times, nothing remarkable takes place. Finally, when I am about to remove the bracelet, something happens and that something is Slice running back into the room so suddenly that I forget to hide the bracelet away.

'What is that on your hand?' He asks, his eyes widening in surprise when he looks at the bracelet. Of course, the first thing he had to notice was this pretty, attention-seeking piece of jewellery.

'Nothing, it's just-' I start but he cuts me off completely.

'Don't lie, I have been warding off whatever it was trying to do to you so now tell me what it is.' He says and that is when I realise why the magic wasn't working. Does this mean that Slice has put some sort of spell on me?

'What have you done? You didn't take my permission to spy on me?' I say sounding ridiculous to my own ears.

'I don't think you need 'permission' to spy on someone genius. Besides I am not spying I am just protecting you.' He says and I struggle with the idea of trusting him blindly.

'Look this is supposed to show me the history, the reason for being a part of this war, you need to put away the spell so that I can get inspired to learn things quickly.' I say, my voice whiny and pathetic.

'Haven't you experienced enough to realise why you need to fight? History is never the reason Selina, you eventually forgive people for their past mistakes, it's the present that makes you fight for the right things in life.' He says and at that moment he seems like he is a hundred years old to me until he shows his toothy grin and sprints towards me, pulling off the bracelet from my wrist and dragging me outside.

'You want reasons right, reasons to fight the Giants and kill them. I will show you those reasons.' He says pulling me along to the corridor and down two flights of stairs. We stop in front of a huge door marked with an F intertwined with a D.

'This hall belongs to the Family of the Deceased, the people who were heartlessly killed by the Giants for the blood to raise that monster.' He says and goosebumps run down my spine.

The face of the nameless girl flashes in front of my eyes and suddenly a shiver runs down my spine. Slice puts his hands around my shoulder, panicking that I would faint again but it's like suddenly I can see the reason why this fight is even more important. It's not just the fact that we will be killed if we don't fight, it's that we will be made into puppets to raise the monster that's slowly rising back to power.

It's a fight for survival. No longer are we the most dangerous organisms roaming on Earth, we have enemies now who threaten to use us to end everything in the world. How wrong was I to not think deeply about Maya's words that minor spirits would be used to raise Asura. As a traitor she was definitely trying to bring me here to deliver my blood in a golden spoon to the monster. I can't even fathom to think what would have happened if my father hadn't questioned her. He must have been using some strong magic to make her spill the truth!

Slice looks at me for an affirmation to step inside and I am so overwhelmed with emotions that I just give the slightest nod of my head. He holds my hand all the while we walk around in the hall, reading stories put up on the doors, of children that were killed by the Giants until a lady walks out of her room. For a minute, she stills on seeing me but then she looks at Slice and her expression turns gloomier before she walks away, not giving us a chance to say a word.

I look at Slice to ask him if he knows her but his face is as white as a sheet and I know immediately that there is a story there.

I gently remove my hand from his and hug him, taking the both of us by surprise, but he is my only friend now and the one person who hasn't betrayed me yet.

'You know that I am waiting for the story, don't you?' I say resuming my position of standing next to him once I feel that he is back to himself but he doesn't reply. He just pulls me along to the door the lady had come out from and that's when I see the photo that brings tears into my eyes. It's a small boy with short blonde hair and blue sparkling eyes. His face is stretched wide into a toothy grin and he doesn't look older than ten.

'This is Koby. He was the sweetest child in this place, a ray of sunshine literally. One day he wanted to go to work with me but I refused. I was working with the hunting army at that time and didn't want him to get injured. Koby wouldn't hear a no. He kept crying about how he wanted to teach the bad guys a lesson but I was firm on my decision. That day Koby was attacked by a Giant. By the time we spotted his body, he was no more. We killed the Giant but when his mother got to know that it was because of me that Koby had ventured off alone, she blamed me, and she still does. I blame me too, he would have been safer with me, I shouldn't have left him alone.' He says, his voice growing heavy with emotions. I hold his hand tightly in silence.

It's not his fault that the little kid died, it is the Giant's and it is wrong of the lady to blame Slice but now is not the time to tell him that. He will argue with me if I say that now but I will tell him sooner or later that he needs to stop blaming himself for somebody else's mistake.

After Slice pays his respects to Koby, we move forward. The place is like a living memoir of all those who died or went missing and every story rages a fire within me. It's not right to kill children or even adults to raise a monster.

The Giants are not doing the right thing! This needs to stop!

'Has there been any communication from the Giant's side or have these attacks been random and do we know who is leading the Giants?' I ask all in one breath to which Slice just laughs.

'The one thing Giants are extremely poor at is communication and obviously, they are not going to warn us about killing people when they desperately need blood for their ultimate master but I have observed that the attacks are strategic. They are attacking a certain age group of people more than others and we can start from there. As for who is leading them, it's still a mystery since every Giant dreams of becoming the King of the clan.' He says and a dream I had forgotten about flashes in front of my eyes.

'Do you think they will attack at the same time ever?' I ask.

'Never, these attacks are like an opportunity to show their power and intelligence. Till we don't kill a majority of them, we are not going to be attacked by a Giant group.' He says and though I feel relieved, the thought that killing children gives their leader power, makes me feel nauseous.

'Do you know any girl that went missing a few days back? Someone who looked a bit like me?' I ask remembering the girl whose body had been found in my village.

Slice looks at me in shock before nodding his head.

'Yes, Kristy, she looked like you from far and I did mistake her for you when I first arrived here. Kristy was- well she was a good person but she was very ambitious. She had been planted here as I later realised to protect you. She had to maintain the aura of an innocent dark-headed girl but she was never good at pretending. She was always true to herself and she felt the need to stand out rather than stay hidden. She was warned multiple times but alas she didn't listen and went missing one day. We got to know what happened with her through your aunt. Thank you for killing Little Bones and taking revenge. Her soul must have been proud of you!' He says and I am confused by my emotions.

On one hand, I want to be sad that someone has been playing a bigger game by planting innocents on my behalf and getting them killed but on the other hand, I also can't help but let out a giggle at the name of the Giant.

'Was he really named Little Bones?' I ask and Slice laughs loudly.

'Well yes, I never paid much thought to his name but now that you point it out, it is indeed funny!' He says laughing a little more.

'Slice, who is planting people to protect me and why are people volunteering?' I ask once the humour is gone and we are left pondering over our thoughts.

'You are more important than you think Selina and there are warriors who are dedicated to protecting humans. They would go to any extent to keep chosen ones like you safe.' He says with sincerity and I feel the weight of his words crushing me.

How many people are aware of the impending war and was I really the last person who got to know about it?

Suddenly my guilt of of killing the two Giants even by mistake evaporates slowly and I feel confident about dealing with the lady from the dream. Mother or not, I will fight my best when she arrives!

XXIV
Twenty Four

Once we come out from the hall, Slice removes a little gadget from his bag and types furiously. After everything, I should not be surprised that he has access to a scientific creation like that but I am. The elders in our village always made it seem like technology was barely present and we were supposed to stay away from it as much as possible but the same message was not passed on to the other villages it seems.

I had seen this gadget once in my younger years in Sehar but had completely forgotten about it until now.

How great would it have been if we were allowed to use this device? Was my lack of touch with technology the reason that my friends never spoke to me? But even Rosa lived in the same village and they spoke to her...

'Selina, a new Giantess has been spotted coming towards our village so I need to leave now, will you agree to stay back today since you haven't received any combat training yet?' Slice asks and I can't help but flinch at how casually he has termed me useless after all the talk of how I am supposed to protect them in the first battle.

I look at him pointedly before snatching his sword from his belt and pointing it at him.

'You will leave me here, only if you want to leave your body too. I will go with you to the fight, after all, she is coming for me.' I say and Slice gives me a huge beam before pulling me down a flight of stairs, to the ground floor, to a huge room marked 'W'.

When we enter inside, I am not disappointed to see that the room is packed with every weapon possible from Guns to Swords. If there are all these weapons why are the Giants still a big danger?

'I know what you must be thinking. All this and yet the fright and incompetence. Well, the Giants also have magic and not all of them can be killed by the same substance. They have some blessings that the Gods had given them long back. We are trying to make a comprehensive list of how each Giant can be killed but there are too many of them. It's like a game of trial and error on the battlefield, only with your lives on the line. I am still amazed by how the two Giants that you killed were the ones with no special blessings. It's truly an immense luck on your side but today it might not be the case. Giantesses usually are masters of manipulation and transfiguration.' Slice says and it sends a shiver down my spine.

'Alright time to leave, follow me.' A tall dark man with closely cropped hair and bleached eyebrows says.

'That's Mic, he is our team leader. Just stay out of his way on the battlefield, he sometimes gets a little too aggressive.' Slice says, giving me a little knife in place of his sword. I nod my head in understanding not taking my eyes off the knife, before we run to follow the rest of the team.

Everyone has a weapon in their hands and I feel like I belong in the troop although no one says anything to me once we start moving towards the target. Moving through the fence, we enter a majorly barren land with a few scattered trees and shrubs.

It seems odd to move in the open but then I spot the flickering around us and see the magic that's hiding us from plain sight.

We walk about five kilometres and find ourselves at the edge of an unknown forest. Well, it's unknown to me but I know that others know it.

'Ok so now we split, I have sent you the coordinates on your devices. We will surround the Giant woman from all sides for better chances of victory. May the spirits of Greog protect us, let's go!' Mic says and immediately Slice pulls me with him. He knows that I can run on my own right? Why does he always pull me this way?

I will have to speak to him about this habit but first, we need to safely kill the lady Giant whose name is still unknown.

We run towards the east, the leaves on the ground crushing under our feet, the wind moving with us making it seem like we are flying. There is an energy buzzing around us and I just know that Slice will need extra protection during the fight to keep us all safe from the worst. His magic is special, it's what's safeguarding our battalion.

Once we reach the destination, I am glad that we are at a little height that would give us some benefit in the fight. We hide behind the trees to spy on our enemy and when we look down we are left speechless by the sight in front of us. It's not a single female but an entire mini army camping out. There are Giants, weird-looking species and also to my surprise humans.

'They have humans in their army.' I whisper to Slice who is just as surprised as I am.

'Are they really?' He whispers back and it's only when I squint a little that I see that there is glamour around the supposed humans. They are all Giants in disguise, capable of infiltrating the villages. How will a handful of us fight so many though?

'Will we really fight all of them right now? It's not wise.' I whisper to Slice but it's like he is in a daze.

I almost look away from him when I notice a small snake on his legs. It's ready to bite him and looks painful with the spines on its body. From when do snakes have spines on them? Without thinking for a second I grab it tightly and pry it away from Slice's leg but it seems like the damage is done because his leg is bleeding profusely from multiple places.

My palms get punctures too because of it's spines but they are the least of my worries at the moment. The snake tries to bite me but it doesn't know that I have handled multiple of its cousins on my expeditions, although always from far! Keeping its mouth as far as possible I use my knife to cut it into two pieces and throw it away.

When I turn towards Slice, I see a strange woman bending towards him and that's when I realise the enemy is aware of our arrival. I push the woman away but it's a huge mistake because her face is horrid with huge cuts bleeding tiny worms making me feel nauseous at the very sight.

At the same time, the snake also decides to come alive and attack me again. I can see the two halves of the body merge back and it's really disgusting. I can't decide what's more horrible the snake or the woman but I need to protect Slice and wake him up before everyone dies and for that, I need to deal with both the monsters. What kind of Giants are these really?

Once the snake is alive, the lady turns to get back to Slice and I feel helpless until an idea strikes me. Well, I am still helpless unless the idea works.

I run towards the lady as soon as the snake is close enough and when I feel it's almost caught up with me I jump away making it lose its control and snap a good portion of the lady's hand away.

I utilise the moment of shock for both the monsters to move Slice out of the lady's reach and while the lady spews profanities at the snake who looks at her in shock I somehow manage to pull him an inch or two away and stand guard in front of him.

Why is it that everyone knows their magic but me? I am truly in a useless position today. The two Giants from earlier seem like a piece of cake in front of these nightmares. From somewhere I hear human screams and I know that we are fighting a losing battle. The Giants' ambush has been successful.

Before long the two monsters turn back to me and the place where the snake had bitten the woman now bleeds worms too like her face. They both look at me, seething in anger and I am left with no choice but to face them with courage no matter how afraid I am from inside.

The lady attacks first and I know better than to cut her so I try to stump her with my knife's butt but she easily grabs my knife and rips it from my hands like a toy before breaking it into tiny pieces.

I stand there paralysed while she laughs at my misery. The snake hisses too as if it's making fun of me. I am left with nothing but leaves to defend Slice. What should I do now?

The snake is the next one to attack me and it comes so fast that I have no time to defend myself. It bites me on the hands, legs and neck and by the time it's done, I know I am dying. I even see an angel come to save me before it all goes dark.

XXV
Twenty Five

The world is dark, lightning and thunder hit the skies continuously and all I see around me is nothing. The ground below me seems hard like it has not seen water for many many days.

My throat is parched and my head hurts but my eyes are sharp like never before. I see some figures fighting in the sky and one of them starts falling down suddenly. I run forward to help in some way but the figure never touches the ground. Right before it can touch the surface, the ground opens up and swallows it and all that's left is the figure's loud ear-piercing screams.

I have to catch myself from falling as the ground swiftly closes again and I can't help but wonder who that person was and who was the person they were fighting with.

At a distance, someone screams my name over and over again and I run to find them when the scene around me starts changing and all I see is a woman bleeding before my eyes are nearly blinded by the sharp light.

'Someone switch off the lights, she is awake.' I hear Papa shout before I feel him holding my hands gently like I am a baby.

Once the lights go out, my eyes open and adjust to the surroundings and the first thing I see is Papa's tired face.

'How? Slice?' I croak out, my voice barely audible, and my throat hurting from the effort.

'Slice is good, thanks to you, but you need to be more careful from now on! How could you just stand there without thinking about your life? You nearly died, do you know how many spells your mother and aunt had to use to keep you alive?' Papa says, his voice soft and emotional.

'How is the rest of the team?' I ask, more like a whisper, to divert his attention from me. I still can't believe how we went there so unprepared and unaware of what we were going to face.

'Selina let's just focus on you okay? You were out for almost a week, you might be hungry, I'll quickly grab some food.' Papa says and tries to leave but I hold onto his hands. He nods his head in a no and I don't even realise when a scream leaves my lips.

It's all my fault. They came to hunt me down and because of me, eight people died, eight people who deserved to live a happy life with their families. Hot tears run down my face and I feel nothing but shame and guilt.

'SelSel, it's not your fault. You all were ambushed. The technology is not working anymore. These are dark times when we can't trust anyone or anything anymore. Let's just say, your mother and I arrived there on time to save you and Slice but from now on we will all have to be careful and alert. The Giants have changed their tactic now after we killed their little army yesterday. They are all coming together now. It's a war. They will be here in four days and we have to be prepared by then. I will get some food now and let your mother and aunt know that you are awake.'

Papa says before kissing me on the forehead and leaving the room.

A shiver runs down my spine just by the thought of how we would fight so many Giants without any aid.

The people here must hate me now. They were told that I would protect them but I am just an extra burden for them.

My mind wanders back to the two monsters that I attempted to fight alone. If they were in the first cohort, how dangerous would be the ones in the remaining army? How many tricks would they know?

If each one needs to be killed in a specific way that means we need at least three people per Giant to win this battle. Even if we get help from Sehar, Tooth and Kholali, it will never be enough. We would be hardly five maybe six hundred people fighting an already lost battle.

No, I can't think this way, especially after everything these people have been through, I have been through. I won't die without fighting, I just won't. We need a proper strategy if we need to win through the trickery. This war was never fair to start with and if we need to win it will have to be by the use of brains, not muscles.

'Selina, you are awake!' Slice enters the room with my mother and aunt and they all look like they have been hit by a bus. There are dark shadows under my mother's and aunt's eyes and Slice has a bruise on his forehead that I fail to remember the story of.

My mother runs her hand through my forehead making me feel lighter before feeding me some food while my aunt holds my right hand tightly and does some magic that automatically makes me feel a hundred percent alright.

'Ma, you and Aunty look exhausted, what's wrong?' I ask my mother as she gets up to put the plates away.

'It's nothing you need to concern yourself with! How could you run away like that from home? Do you know what would have happened if we hadn't found you guys, you would be dead! I didn't wait a hundred years for a child to only have her die at the hands of a snake and a cursed one.' My mother yells at me and instead of feeling sad, I actually feel happy to hear her scold me. No matter how odd but it helps me feel normal.

'Why are you smiling like an idiot?' My mother says before giving me a hug and lots of kisses on the face.

'You can take today to get better but tomorrow you need to find a way to trigger your magic. Forces are not coming in from Sehar and we need all the help we can get.' My mother says finally before leaving with my aunt to get back to her task of what I assume is taking care of the injured.

Slice just stands there looking at me in concern like I would disappear any moment.

Once my mother and aunt leave, he sits on the chair my father was sitting on earlier. He looks tensed and angry and I wonder what the reason is.

'They refused to help us!' He says in a whisper and goosebumps cover my skin.

'My own father refused to send his army and the elders are also missing, how can they all desert us at this time?' He cries out while I sit there in shock absorbing all the information he has just given me.

How could they all leave us to fend for ourselves? If the giants pass through, they all will be dead too! Everyone is working so hard here to protect the last bit of humankind but they want to give it up, no there has to be some other reason, I can't think otherwise at least until the Giants are gone.

'Slice, I know you are sad, but there is no time to feel sorrow or betrayal right now. Please teach me how to fight, how to bring out the magic I have that everyone keeps talking about.' I say, my voice breaking a little from the guilt and fear of not being the powerful force that everyone has been made to believe in.

Slice just nods before helping me get out of bed and to his room where the stuff I have been provided with is. He is unusually quiet on the way but I don't know how to break the silence without talking about things that would upset him further.

Once Slice leaves, I quickly change into a fresh pair of clothes and take a moment to look at the sky and say a small prayer. If the Gods are looking down at this mess, they should know we need their help to fight the monsters they once fought.

They need to share their knowledge with us, after all, their blessings have been turning into curses time and again!

'If you are listening to me God, watching us all in our misery, please help us. Most nature spirits won't help us in this battle, unless we show them we are going to win, because they are scared. Please reveal my powers to me, the very ones you promised would be useful!' I shout out, tears flowing through my eyes.

I close my eyes in despair for a second and go out of the room to join Slice but only there is no Slice or the chamber there anymore. I turn around to go back into the room, but the door has disappeared too. Great, so the Giants have not only already reached Greog, but they have started playing their mind games too.

The place is covered in snow, it's freezing cold and combined with the winds, it seems like a gateway to hell. I scream for help, but there is no one around. I start walking slowly against the wind to keep myself warm, but it doesn't help much.

I have almost given up when I hear the sound of bells behind me. Slowly turning around, I am shocked to see a cow. Cows have been extinct for quite some time now, how is one standing here in this temperature?

It starts walking towards me and I stand there still, not wanting to enrage it but it just walks past me, a voice in my head saying,' Follow me!'

Did I hear that or was it my imagination?

XXVI
Twenty Six

As I walk behind the cow, I can't help but wonder how foolish I am being. Who follows a cow that has appeared out of nowhere? The voice I heard has to be an imagination since no animal other than humans speaks.

As I deliberate on whether I should continue walking or not, the cow abruptly stops and I almost collide with it. What happens next is something I had not imagined in my wildest dreams although by now I should always expect the unexpected. The cow turns into a man. Not just any man, a man whose face is sparkling and young.

'I am Lord Nandi's chosen one, my name is Swarn, it's a pleasure to meet you!' He says extending his hand towards me as I stand there in a daze. Lord Nandi's chosen one? As far as I have heard Lord Nandi was the most trusted aid and also the vehicle of God Shiva. He was never one of those lords with a palace or a huge army but still to keep my life intact, I shake hands with the beautiful 'chosen one'.

'I know you must be having doubts but times have changed and the myths have remained stuck to the very beginning of everything.' He says with a short laugh.

'The Gods have needed more security with the changing times and Lord Nandi recruits the best warriors of each era for this noble duty. When he saw me changing into an ox, he immediately contacted me, however, let's not digress, I come bearing a message from my boss.' He says while I cringe at how I ignorantly thought that he is a cow, I should have paid more attention in the history class but alas!

'So my boss heard your scream, obviously, you were so loud we all heard you, but yeah, although sir Nandi didn't like you blaming the Gods, he empathises with you and so he has asked me to tell you this:

'When you conquer your feelings and control the emotions that run like a river through your mind, you shall become who you are destined to be!' Hmph that was hard to remember but this is your message, if you want me to repeat it again, I will but I am sure you are smart and must have memorised it in a single go!' He says with a smile that's insanely peaceful for times like these.

He seriously came all the way to tell me this, another piece of a cryptic, nonsensical message? Why even bother to reply when you want to talk in circles?

'Do you possibly have any other piece of valuable information for me, that might be useful in a battle that's almost about to begin?' I ask but he just stands there in shock.

'You think that what I told you just now is not important? Do you realise if you actually follow the advice, how great you would become? Sir Nandi had given me a similar message in the last century and look where I am now. Yes, it took me a century but I am an ox, we have the least developed brains out of all the other magical creatures. You are a -you are much more powerful I mean. You can figure it out if you think about it. And see the bonus, the Gods will help you fight the dark one once you defeat the Giants and your friends succeed in their mission. It's so much motivation right there, you get to fight under the guidance of the Gods themselves, it's a dream come true for warriors like us who have never gotten this opportunity despite serving for centuries.' He says with a huge smile before waving his hand in front of my face and suddenly I am back in Slice's room.

I am a what? He was so close to telling me and then he had to wake up out of his trance and send me back with nothing but a few words of wisdom that would have probably not worked even if we had more time.

But that's the problem we don't have any time at all!

I angrily throw a cushion down from Slice's bed and it only makes me feel guilty. I should be thankful to Lord Nandi for at least giving some reaction. I can't comprehend the fact that the Gods will help to fight the dark one only once we defeat the Giants, what kind of a game is this? And who are these friends of mine who are on a mission? What is this mission and how is this all fair?

We might all die anyway if we don't defeat the Giants which is what seems to have a 99.9999% probability at the moment. How do I bring my emotions under check?

Taking a deep breath, I open the door again and this time I indeed come out in the right hallway.

'Took your time didn't you? Let's hurry now, we have a lot scheduled ahead of us today.' Slice says before running up the stairs. This time we only go up one floor before Slice does something in the air and we land on a terrace.

The view is amazing around me. Blue skies, green forests, people just doing their everyday routines, if only we weren't getting prepared for war, I would have loved to spend hours just sitting here looking at nothing in particular.

'Come and sit down over here.' Slice calls out and I find him sitting cross-legged on a mat on the floor. Really? I thought we were going to practice fighting. Not wanting to waste time arguing and playing question-answer rounds I just quickly walk towards him and sit down in the same manner as him.

'Well, that was easier than expected.' Slice says with a smirk and I give him a hard tap on the head to get him to focus again.

'That was not needed.' He says rubbing the spot where I hit him before joining his hands together and holding him to his chest.

'Copy me and close your eyes.' He says and I follow his instructions.

'Think about everything you are feeling, the breeze, the emotions locked up in your heart, the heat of the Sun and bring it in front of your eyes. See it through and through. Sort through the images and take this time to heal from the burn of these feelings.' He says and although it feels weird to picture myself being able to do it, I try following his words. After all, they are not very different from what Lord Nandi told me through Swarn.

Mustering as much concentration as I can, I reach out to the deepest corner of my mind to bring out emotions but it feels too dark and dangerous. The mere thought of opening those boxes I had tucked away day after day when Rosa had gone missing scares me. Those are the emotions I never want to feel again- misery, guilt, pain, the rawness of tackling a bereavement when you felt you were responsible, the joy of finding your dead best friend only to realise she hates you, the fear of encountering a Giant and killing it- no its too much, I can't feel it all again.

My head hurts and although I feel the breeze and the Sun, I can't deal with the memories right now. Nausea rises through my throat and when I open my eyes, it's only to find Slice looking at me in horror.

Did he feel what I felt? Did he realise I am a coward? Will he go and tell the villagers now that I am useless? Tears seep down my eyes as I run to a corner of the terrace and lie crunched, throwing out my guts. The words and images float around my head all the while making me shiver despite the hot weather.

Someone pats my back as I sob like a loser who can't even battle her emotions. As days pass the cloud of gloom and despair, hanging on my head, is only growing bigger. This is not how I need to be at the moment.

I need to have a clear head to concentrate and for that, I need to face my fears. Shivering I slowly get up as the hand holds onto me. It makes me realise that I will never fall unless I give in. When I wipe my eyes and turn around there is no one and Slice is still sitting at his spot but I feel stronger now.

Quickly cleaning my face with the towel near my seat and rinsing my mouth with the water from a tap on the other side of the terrace that Slice guides me to, I take my seat again, this time ready to win, that is until I close my eyes and find myself standing in front of the Bleeding Man. Wrists held by creepers and no one around except for the monster who started this mess.

XXVII
Twenty Seven

'I really can't believe they chose youuuu, its pathetic reallyyyy!' The Bleeding Man says his voice cutting through my ears, his aura making me feel haunted and on fire not as much as the first time I met him which makes the scenario scarier but this time I refuse to be afraid.

No, how dare he enter my mind and try to scare me like this. I concentrate on the creepers holding my hands while he continues to mock the Gods for choosing me, sometimes mentioning my parents.

I can feel the thorns of the creepers pinching me and when I try to move my wrists, they attack my hands more viciously. I wish I could make my hands thinner but I know that is not possible. What else can I do? If only I had someone with me that could distract these creepers!

Stop with the wishful thinking Selina, you have to do something. You can't let this disgusting creature mock you like this. The more time I waste in thinking, the more fun Asura has. His insults start getting more broad range and land on Slice.

'Oh, that friend of yours, I must say he is a fool for not listening to your other friendsss! He thinks you will remember your powers. He thinks he can rely on you despite being let down by his own fatherrr!' Asura says, laughing so loudly that I feel my ears go numb. With my hearing finally gone, I can just see his lips moving but thankfully no disturbing sounds enter my ears and the newfound peace makes me think faster.

What can cause the creepers to move back? Closing my eyes, I try to feel them again, they hold me in anger as if I have offended them in the past.

'Hello, creepers!' I say in my mind as if they can hear me but if there is magic out there then I want to give it a chance before I accept that I have gone crazy from the poison coming out of the Bleeding Man.

For a few seconds, nothing happens except for my ears feeling really hot like the last time but then a distant voice replies.

'Hello blessed one!' A young boy says, his voice is soft yet prickly like the thorns.

'Can you please stop holding me so tightly? I need your cooperation please, I need to do something, I can't just stand here and let Asura insult my family like that.' I plead, my voice sounding sugary even though I am speaking in my mind.

'Hmm, why should I help you? Your species has only ever hurt mine! Did you know that your aunt once sliced through my father's aunt? It's a famous story, that one, amongst my kingdom. A witch slicing through the king's sister.' He says sounding almost bored.

Who knew that even plants had their kingdoms and way of communicating but then at this point, nothing is impossible is what I need to keep reminding myself.

'Mr Creeper or should I say Your Highness, I officially would like to apologise to you on behalf of my aunt and all my fellow human beings for the stupidity that we have shown in the past by hurting your breed. Will you please join us in this battle? Your support will never be forgotten if we win.' I say trying my best to understand his point of view and portraying a genuine grievance.

'Ha, who knew a day would come when the humans would ask for our forgiveness? You have impressed me but how do I know you mean what you just said?' He says his voice going from excited to bored like a well-known singer changing notes.

'Well, how would you like me to promise you?' I ask knowing full well that I have made a grave error by asking the question. He is on the enemy team, I shouldn't have given him the liberty straight away.

'A drop of your blood would be all.' He says his voice having an edge of victory. What if this is his scheme?

I have heard of rituals where willingly giving blood can give someone the power to control you. It's the most common threat parents would give children who asked about the Tooth Village.

'No, because I can sense that you want to trick me. You want my apologies but you don't want to act fair yourself, how can anyone trust you and not hurt you because of this behaviour? If you want the world to accept you and not cut you as it does now, you need to change your ways as well.' I say, my heart beating fast from the anticipation of the repercussions of the creeper.

'Ha, you amaze me again. Fine, you have me in your team, I will let you go, for now, also because I want to see what you can do unrestrained. No one can hurt Asura but I want to see your attempt.' It says laughing and suddenly true to his words, the creepers holding my hands suddenly slide away.

I open my eyes to see Asura looking at me like an experiment that has worked well. My ears stop feeling hot and the scenery shifts again, I am back on the roof now with Slice beaming at me.

'Well done, no one has ever managed to make Mr. Creeper do what they want, but you succeeded. Now do you believe in yourself? Not everything has to be magic Selina. Your power is the way you speak.' Slice says looking extremely pleased with himself but I feel offended.

How did he know all those things that had the potential to hurt me? Why did he enter my mind without taking my permission that too with Mr Creeper as a companion? Does he see me as an experiment, a way to get the things that he and everyone else want and then discard in the corner? Is that why he rescued me and is that why he is so pressed upon keeping me alive?

'Selina, what's wrong? Are you okay? You did really well today, you don't need to overthink. We can practice every day till you become a master at controlling your thoughts.' He says sounding extremely happy at his achievement like he scored full marks in a test.

'Slice, you had no right to enter my mind like that! Why did you do it without my permission? Tell me did you read through all my memories and emotions to do your homework in order to act like Asura?' I say my voice shaking with anger. I know he is trying to help but this is not the right manner.

He stares at me in shock before looking disappointed not in himself but me.

'Really? I am trying to help you here, help you prove to everyone that you are worthy of being a chosen one and all you can think about is yourself. This is a war Selina, there are going to be no boundaries here and if you don't get a grip on your emotions and mind, anyone will be able to enter your mind and make you do things you don't want to do. Trust me when I say that I have no interest in going through your memories or the vivid sob stories in your head but if I am given a task I will do it well so if the only way to train you is this, I will do it, no matter how many times I have to!' He says before getting up to go away but I am not going to let him after what he just said.

How dare he put the blame on me? I never asked to be a chosen one and yet I am trying my best to navigate blindly through a path I have no clue of. I thought he would be by my side and tell me the truth always but he is also just like them.

'So Mr. Mind reader I am sure you must know what's going on in my head so let me save my breath and just say that if you ever come near me again, it won't be good for you. I will help my best in this war, but you and I are no longer acquaintances.' I say and run away leaving him standing shocked at my unexpected comeback.

No one has a right to enter my mind like that, no one! I need to find a way of contacting Swarn again, he is the only one who can help me in an ethical manner. But how do I reach out to him again?

'Swarn if you can hear me, please show me a way to connect with you again. I really need your help!' I say like a small prayer while looking at the sky before climbing down a flight of stairs and landing in a strange pink room.

XXVIII
Twenty Eight

I look around, my senses on high alert. What type of room is this? Not just the walls but even the light is pink and the brightness gives me a slight headache. I am honestly tired after all the events that have unfolded since the Giant trap and landing in a surprise room was truly the last thing on my bucket list.

I try to think of ways to escape when I feel it, a slight dip in the air behind me. Trusting my instincts I move away immediately and when I turn around I don't know who is more shocked.

'So you are indeed getting better then. Slice is a good teacher, patient, and better than me definitely. I am proud.' He says, a small smirk playing around his lips.

'Jackson, what are you doing here? Where have you brought me?' I demand but he pretends like he has all the time in the world, setting his slightly dishevelled hair which is dyed a weird shade of purple and adjusting the collar of his neon green shirt.

'Ahh, were you speaking to me sweety? Well for starters, I am tired of playing messenger between my wife and her mother and I need some entertainment but coming to real reasons, your new friend sent me here to help you. By the way, why do you never call me directly, why is it different people asking me always?' He says with a groan, now playing with the rings on his fingers and adjusting them to match his outfit.

'My new friend? You mean Slice?' I ask slightly confused. I haven't made any friends here. Wait a minute does he know Swarn? He can't possibly be referring to Swarn, can he?

The look he gives me in response makes it clear that he is indeed talking about Swarn but when did they get time to discuss my case and decide that I need Jackson's help?

'Look little girl, I am your best shot at the moment considering everyone else is either pissed, too busy or trying to get back in your friend list. We don't have much time but I can see that you have made progress and I am happy with that. I can teach you how to master your skills and I can teach you and Slice how to use your powers in unison to create the kind of energy that's needed to defeat an army of Giants. Cool? Let's begin.' He says as if he wasn't asking but telling me everything like a statement of purpose.

'I haven't agreed and you haven't asked Jackson? How can I even trust you after what Maya did? I am glad my parents made it here with my aunt, safely too I might add but Maya almost got everyone killed.' I say and he starts to look angry. Great, one more hater is about to get added to my list of people who don't like me.

'Look, Selina, I am not Maya nor do I take accountability for her actions but this time I can say that she had a very good reason for what she did. Besides I was there and I wouldn't have let you die for sure but had we not allowed

Asura to reach you, our daughter would have been no more and that would have led to an apocalypse led by Maya's anger. So it's time to let go of grudges and start afresh.' He says, and I don't know whether to trust him or not.

'You said you were playing messenger between Maya and her mother. How do I know that you are still on our side and not Maya's? After all your daughter can fall into danger again, and you might stand aside with Maya to watch Asura destroy us all!' I say unafraid of how he would react and he goes still, so much so that I almost feel that he is frozen.

'Look, our daughter is safe now and will no longer be a hindrance for me in this war. Besides, I know Maya is also on our team, it's just that she was afraid the last time. So please let's not waste more time and begin.' He says in an unrealistically calm voice and I decide to let go of the matter for now.

'Hello, I am Jackson, your teacher and one of the most powerful forces of nature in the world.' He says extending his hand towards me and looking ridiculous with the forced expression on his face.

Schooling my features and forcing my friendly self to take the lead, I repeat his gesture.

'Hello, I am Selina, a used-to-be normal girl.'

My words make him laugh and I feel glad to see someone finding me amusing after everything. What worries me is how today's events would affect my friendship with Slice especially since we are supposed to be working together. I am also glad that he isn't here to read my thoughts.

Wait, what if it's Slice again, pretending to be Jackson?

'Slice if it's you, please get out of my brain, I think I told you not to use this magic a few minutes back.' I say looking at Jackson but his confused face tells me what I need to know.

'Are you saying that Slice can enter your mind and show you the things he wants you to see? Humph, he could never do that spell when I was teaching it to him, I wonder what changed.' Jackson says after a minute or two and I continue to stand in silence not willing to overshare in the said person's absence.

'How long did it take you to teach Slice and how do you plan to guide me? Also, I don't think Slice would like to train with me so...' I say but Jackson just grins like an idiot.

'Slice was an easy student, very aware of his powers and eager to absorb everything that I said, you on the other hand are difficult. You still don't believe in half the things that people tell you and you most definitely don't know how to read people and understand who is your friend and who is your foe.' He says, evading my questions partly. His answer makes me feel irritated and uncomfortable but it's also true, partly might I add.

'When do we start?' I say abruptly to change the topic and get rid of the unwanted attention on me.

'We start now of course unless you are too tired but bear in mind that I am paid by the minute so you have already wasted quite a lot of Swarn's money in talking to me.' He says with a toothy grin that I want to punch out of his face.

'You couldn't have mentioned that earlier and why the heck is Swarn paying you? I thought you both were friends?' I ask flabbergasted at the thought of Swarn's hard-earned money going to waste because of me.

'Well, I never said that we are friends, I said your new friend to be specific but obviously, you don't pay attention to detail. He is your friend and he is paying for you to learn to fight your own battles. He can't come running at your beck and call. He is a busy guy.' He says and I slap my forehead in my mind for assuming things.

'Let's begin then?' I ask as Jackson stares at me in complete silence and before I can say another word, I find myself lying on the ground groaning in pain.

How did I not see this coming? Of course, this would be the first thing that he would do. This is all he did the last time and teachers always begin with a revision of the last class. Why am I so dumb?

A hand shoots in front of my face but I ignore it taking my time to stand as Jackson basks in victory. As he does a little spin to celebrate his win, I stick out my leg and then it's time for the pupil to shine and the teacher to groan.

'Well done, well done, so you do remember lesson one although I might add that a little revision was essential. In a real battlefield you would be dead by now so stop smiling.' He says once he gets up and I can't help but smile wider at his misery.

'Admit it, Jackson, you are a sore loser.' I say and this time he laughs with me.

'Alright, alright, let's move to lesson number two, let's see how well Slice has taught you. You could feel the dip in air pressure but now you have to learn how to differentiate the most important factors from the ones that have been created to distract you. Tell me what do you feel?' He says and I can't help but feel pressured.

I try to concentrate on the air around me but the distinct buzzing sound distracts me from focusing as I use my energy to focus only on the air, the sound grows louder and before I know it I am lying flat on my face.

'Lesson number two is don't ignore the most evident to focus on the things you don't know.' Jackson says and when I open my eyes I find myself in a bed, more precisely in the infirmary bed with my mother staring down at my face.

XXIX
Twenty Nine

'Welcome back!' My mother says, her voice full of sarcasm and I wince at the throbbing in my head that I realise was not there before.

'Did I not tell you specifically to take a rest today? Of course, your head is going to hurt. Even though you didn't do much physical training, mental training takes a deeper toll on your body, do you understand that now?' She says and I groan remembering she can read my thoughts loud and clear.

Once I mumble an apology for not listening to her, my mother runs her hand through my head and I find the pain gone, just like that although I find her looking pale.

'Ma, are you alright? Why are you doing this magic when it leaves you feeling sick?' I ask feeling guilty for making her weak.

'For the greater purpose. We need every person right now and if this magic helps to get them back on their feet quickly, I will do it. Don't worry about me, I am taking enough precautions and I have herbs that can help rejuvenate me whenever my power sources are running low. But you need to be careful SelSel. I know that there has been a lot of pressure put on you but you have to be you, never forget yourself to become the person everyone wants you to be. Even they don't know what they want you to be, okay?' My mother says and although I don't feel a hundred percent convinced about her health, her words about being me make me feel happy.

It's true indeed that only my parents really care about me. Everyone else just sees me as someone who might save them from the Giants but I can't blame them. It's all about survival now.

My mother leaves after giving me some hot food to eat and as I sit there and nibble on the food, savouring its taste, I see Slice entering the room.

'I am sorry.' He says the moment he comes closer to me but I don't know how to trust him. I am at the crossroads I was when I first met him in Gionia.

'I know that I should have asked your permission Selina, but do you think you would have been able to react the same way you did if you would have known my skill? I know that no one likes to see someone in their head without permission but I had to do it, Selina. However, I have no excuse for my behaviour afterwards. I said some things that were in the poorest taste and I apologise for them with my heart.' He says and I know that even though I forgive him, I will never forget nor trust him again.

'It's ok Slice, I know now that it's a war zone and everyone is going to be doing things they find are needed to be done to win. I can see how much everyone wants me to change and become something that no one including me knows what is but you all need to understand that I was in the shadows for so long that I didn't even know of this trouble until a few days back. There is not much time left but I promise I am doing my best here to become what the prophecy says I would be. Now it will be nice if you leave me to rest. I think I have had enough for today. I will see you in the training with Jackson.' I say and turn away from Slice.

I feel him standing next to me for a long time wanting to say something but ultimately he decides against it and leaves me alone with unsaid words hanging in the already dense atmosphere.

Slice

I shouldn't have done it. I shouldn't have said those words to her but her memories made me agitated.

Going into someone's head comes with a price and that price is feeling the dread of their horrors, the guilt of their mistakes and the pain of their injuries. With Selina, I felt all three.

Who would have known that one teenage girl was feeling such a mental burden? But if going inside her head and shouldering some of that pain meant helping her feel a little stronger, I would do it again and again and again.

Even when we were little, I couldn't help but look after her. Of course that meant pretending to look after Rosa because where Rosa was Selina was, those two were like two peas in a pod. Selina was immensely independent and strong-willed and I often found myself staring at the way she handled things. Her brilliance and self-assurance inspired me to have courage in the darkest times.

Seeing her in distress, feeling what she was carrying in her little head all this time, made me feel angry for not helping her sooner. Yes, she hates me now and I know that she will never trust me again but I would rather have her hate than see her on the brink of death again.

બ૦

When I get up, my mind is surprisingly clear and the thoughts that had been troubling me all these days seem to be at bay. I don't know how this has happened but a clear mind is good. Getting up, I decide to leave but realise that I don't know where exactly I can go.

'You are up finally.' A voice says startling me for a moment and I realise it's Jackson.

He is standing there, his hair coloured a new shade of blue and his expression the complete opposite of the peace that colour blue brings.

'Jackson, is it time for training?' I ask immediately getting up. I am surprised to see that my clothes are changed and I am wearing a fresh black top and Fabric X trousers. Fabric X is the material used to make clothes for the army. It's a warm orange color material that is resistant to almost everything though I am unsure if it is resistant to magic or Giants. Only a special weaver in the Sehar knows how to make this fabric and has access to the technology used to replicate it. I wonder who changed me and how the people here got access to Fabric X.

'We will go to train but first you need to help Slice. He took half of your pain when he entered your mind and now he is weak. You need to help him by balancing the emotions between the two of you.' Jackson says leaving me confused. Slice took half of my painful emotions? How did he do that and why did he do that? Is he so desperate for me to find my true self that now he feels it's necessary for him to burden my emotional baggage even if it hurts him?

'C'mon, it's time to go.' Jackson says pulling me along and I move with purpose. A purpose to give Slice a piece of my mind. We go through the corridor and climb up a flight of stairs to end up in front of a door that is extremely familiar to me. When we enter, I see Slice lying on the bed, his eyes closed and face red.

Sitting beside him, I take hold of his hand to wake him up but I am shocked to see how feverishly hot it is.

'We need to take him to the infirmary, he is sick.' I tell Jackson but when I turn back he is no longer there.

'Where did you disappear?' I ask angrily but all I get is silence.

'Selina, why-what are you doing here?' I hear Slice ask, his voice no louder than a murmur and turn to see that he is trying to get up.

'Just lie still ok, what is wrong with you? How could you steal my emotions like that? Is this war so important to you that you want to die before you even kill a Giant?' I ask my voice quivering. No matter what, he is still my childhood friend and I can't see him die.

'Not the war, you, you are important Selina. If you would have gone out again with the pain and guilt, you would have died in the first five minutes. Some of the Giants out there are masters of playing with emotions.' He replies and I am shook with his words. Does he really care about me as a person?

'I- how can I help? Jackson said we have to balance this weight you are carrying alone.' I ask not wanting to think deeply about his words no matter how positively they affect me after everything.

'No, you- I can handle it, I just need some time to sort everything and put it in a box.' He says trying to remove his hand from my grip. Does he really think I am going to let him do this?

'Fine then, we can stay here for as long as you refuse to speak and give the solution. Let everyone fight alone, there is no hurry.' I say lying down next to him, holding his hand even more tightly than before.

'Selina- fine I can see how adamant you have become the minute your head has become clear again. I will try to give you back some pain OK, but that would mean that I need to enter your mind again, will you be fine with me doing that?' He says turning a little to look at me.

'No- and not because I don't want you in my head- I mean of course I don't want that but you trying to do that will take up energy. I know that doing these tricks is hard. There has to be another way.' I say and he just groans.

'Fine then the next way is that we both need to sit facing each other and concentrate on the energy between us. This will bring out the emotions from inside me to balance out the low energy on your end.' He says and although it sounds difficult, I agree with it.

Thirty

I prop up the pillows around Slice and help him sit up. Seeing him in so much distress because of me is unbearable. Once he is able to sit up, I hold his hand and sit opposite him waiting for him to gain the strength to give me the next instructions.

'Focus on my aura and try to pull some of the black light surrounding it.' He says, his voice like a whisper.

At first, his request seems vague. How can I see his aura? But then I think about how I see people to understand their character and mentality and the more I look at him, the more I start seeing the light around him. There is a dim fog surrounding the bright aspects, almost choking the brightness and coercing darkness to form all around him.

I concentrate on the fog, holding Slice's hand even more tightly as if that would help me pull the fog towards me. The more I stare at it the more I feel like I am moving towards it, the minute I am about to touch it something happens and I find myself falling however Slice's hand holds me back.

The sensations continue to make me feel dizzy until my eyes suddenly open and I find Slice staring back at me, our hands still clasped tightly, a faint pink covering his cheeks. His body temperature seems normal but what is abnormal is the slight buzz in my head that seems like an external noise.

It's almost like I can hear someone's thoughts but the radio frequency is bad and I need to be closer to the source to hear distinctly. I try to concentrate to hear better but there is a sharp buzz in my head like the door is shut on my face when I try to enter through.

'Selina, are you ok?' Slice asks when I wince audibly, his voice sounding more powerful than even before he felt sick.

'Yeah, what happened? I feel different somehow and there is a small buzzing in my head.' I say. Slice coughs a little before tucking some loose strands of my hair behind my ear.

'In taking some of my bad energy, you aligned our minds, Selina. We are sharing our energy now.' He says, his face not giving away his feelings.

'So you mean, if my energy runs low, I can take some of yours, like a common energy reservoir between us?' I say and he nods his head.

'There's more isn't it?' I say knowing it can't be something as simple as sharing energy.

'We are each other's energy reservoirs but at the same time, if something happens to either of us, the other will also be in a lot of pain and might never recover in case of death.' Slice says with a grim face.

'Oh no, why didn't you tell me this before Slice, I would never-' I start saying but Slice just shushes me.

'Look, I knew the risks but it's better this way. I would know when to come and help you when you are in trouble and you would know too if something goes downhill for me.' He says and I don't know how to process the information. Why is he so keen to die for me?

'If you guys are done forming an energy bond, it's time to practice.' Jackson says appearing out of nowhere and making me jump in surprise. My sudden motion scares Slice too who pulls me behind himself in a protective gesture and gives a groan when he sees it's only Jackson.

I didn't realise that the effect of the energy transfer would be so quick. Slice already looks stronger than before.

'Ah the joys of close friendships, I miss those days when we were this noble that we would protect our best friends from danger.' Jackson says in a dreamy voice and I can't help but feel alert at his words.

'Do you mean you would let others die if it meant keeping yourself alive? Then how are you on our side?' I ask but Jackson only laughs.

'Don't pay attention to him, Selina, Jackson has a habit of being dramatic. He was the one who inspired Shakespeare to write the famous Brutus scene.' Slice says, getting up from the bed and wearing his shoes.

'Who is Shakespeare?' I ask unable to control my curiosity. Most of the things were destroyed after the Great Climatic Revenge and now we can only learn about the past through stories and by investing in old artefacts. Of course, the king has a good collection of old books and gadgets but most of us still aspire to learn about them, touch them and dream about the world before.

On my question, both Slice and Jackson look outraged.

'You really don't know who Shakespeare is?' Jackson asks while Slice has the decency to mask his expressions and look unbothered.

'Well, not all of us have lived a thousand years or were born in a family where we could afford artefacts and old books. Also, the last time I heard this name it was from

Maya. Who is this Brutus guy anyway?' I say crossing my arms. Jackson laughs while Slice just brings a book from a shelf in the right corner of his room that I had never seen before.

'Here, this is the book that has the character, Brutus, we were talking about. The book is called Julius Caesar. You can read it in your free time.' Slice says giving me the small book, and I can't help but be fascinated but its antiquity. It has a royal maroon colour with a golden inscription. The book is light and at first glance looks like a mini rule book but the feel of it brings a different kind of serenity in me. It smells amazing too and I can't wait to start reading it.

'Thank you so much, Slice, for giving me this ancient wonder. I can't wait to find out who Brutus is.' I say and Slice just nods before handing me a sword which is quite beautiful too.

It is sleek with leaves rising from the hilt. The hilt itself is wooden and fits perfectly into my grip. The weight of the sword is perfect too and I find myself swinging it like I have been doing it for ages.

'OK, I didn't expect the sword to become your friend this fast but I am happy for you. The sword will help you fight those honourable Giants that don't like to use magic and even those that do not have any magic per se.' Slice says while Jackson just stands there nodding proudly at his words. He looks like a teacher who has realised his efforts have paid off.

'How do I fight the ones who know magic though? We saw in our last fight that they don't attack independently but in groups of mixed varieties?' I ask, suddenly not so happy about my lack of power.

'The energy reservoir.' Jackson says while Slice looks a little offended at Jackson's sudden words as if it were a secret I wasn't supposed to know.

'Why do you think this one over here'-he continues pointing at Slice who looks anywhere but at us- 'isn't that upset over being energy bonded to you. He has magic and you have your spirit. You both will fight in a pair and I am sure you will work out the mind barriers by the time of war to communicate without words.' He says and I am surprised to realise that I wasn't that far off when I thought about the buzzing in my head.

'So, you can't teach me any magic?' I ask and Jackson shakes his head leaving me disappointed.

'Well, you haven't shown any signs yet and you can't be taught magic unless you have been blessed at birth.' He says quietly before clicking his fingers and lo and behold our surroundings change. No longer are we standing in Slice's room but we are on the terrace where Slice and I were practicing earlier.

I squint my eyes to confirm if we are really on the terrace or if Jackson is playing his mind games. A butterfly suddenly flies towards me and before it can reach me I squat down to avoid its attack. I am not sure why I do that but it is an instinct that I can't avoid.

'How did you know that you needed to avoid that butterfly?' Slice says, now holding the butterfly in a glass cage.

'I- I don't know but in the past whenever I have dreamed the butterfly has never been my friend and so it was just one of those gut reactions, you know?' I say and he nods, his expression masked like he is pondering over my words.

'Well this is a spy butterfly, in fact, she isn't just a spy she is someone you know really well.' He says while the butterfly now impatient starts flying furiously in her cage.

'Let her out Slice.' Jackson says, his eyes focused on the little creature.

The minute Slice opens the cage, Jackson makes a little gesture and a girl falls with a groan.

XXXI
Thirty One

'Rosa?' I ask surprised to see my ex-best friend lying on the ground, a huge gash on her face and her lips quivering. Her dress is a little tethered and worn out and she looks like she had looked when she had been let out from Thornos.

Jackson is frozen in his place which is a surprise considering he is always spirited unless Maya is around and Slice looks agitated.

'Why are you here Rosa? Do you not understand that you are being tracked and you can bring unnecessary trouble here?' Slice asks, standing with his arms crossed, his body angled suddenly in a way that it looks like he is shielding me.

'I am sorry Slice for endangering your little safe space but let me tell you that you risked everyone here the minute you saved her! M-my place was tracked the minute she left and my friends- I don't even know where they are anymore!' She shrieks.

'What do you mean Rosa?' Slice asks, his voice now concerned.

'It means exactly what I said, the prophecy was true, she is not our friend, she is the enemy and you are shielding her. Trub has also been caught since he met her. She is not our ally Slice, why can't you see that? I had just come here to warn you, and if I am not welcome to stay, I will leave immediately.' She says, her eyes glistening with unshed tears.

I can't believe that after all this time, she still thinks I am a spy from some prophecy, some black dot on her future that will lead to her death. How did one prophecy make her believe such things about me immediately despite our long friendship?

I look at Slice and Jackson who seem to be lost in deep thoughts. Are they silently agreeing to her words through some magical mental link?

'Well, if Rosa wants to stay and help, we shouldn't turn her away, should we?' I say, making Jackson and Slice look at me in shock. Even Rosa looks surprised at my suggestion. What option do I even have, either I could have stood there like a depressed fool who relies on other's opinions or I could have taken the lead and walked away with my head held high. I chose the latter.

I turn and walk away from the trio as fast as my little feet can take me. Despite everything, there isn't a single person who can vouch for me immediately. *What about the fact that they form energy bonds with you,* a small part of my mind says and I instantly regret my actions. Was I too melodramatic in walking away like that?

I shouldn't have done it. What if Jackson and Slice were thinking of some important questions to ask her or a plan to find out what she is up to by coming to Greog? I can't believe how stupid and emotional I am these days! One prick of the thorn and I am either sobbing or trying to chop down the flower from the stem.

However, regardless of my behaviour, what always amazes me is how deeply everyone here knows each other's powers like they have known each other for ages. Is it possible that while I was sent back to my village, others were undergoing training? What if Rosa had never been captured but secretly sent to practice her powers? And was it Rosa who had led me to that Giant when Slice had taken me to that Room 'X'?

No, I can't waste my time thinking about the unknown. I need to concentrate on making strategies and learning about the different Giants we might face in the war.

I am so lost in my thoughts that I don't even realise I have entered an unknown chamber. It is dimly lit and has a different aura around it. While the rest of the chambers in this building are bright and homely despite the huge corridors, this place looks like it is used to torture people.

Go away, Selina. This place is not for you.

A voice suddenly whispers in my ears, leaving me cold and alert.

'Who is here? Who are you? Reveal yourself!' I scream only to be met with silence. I slowly move forward, wary of anyone attacking me but despite all my precautions, I take one wrong step and find myself tumbling down into a dark mysterious world.

I scream for what it's worth but the hole is so deep I wonder if anyone even heard me.

I fall onto a wet muddy floor, my hands and legs bleeding from the rough slide. I have barely stopped feeling dizzy when I hear the words that shock me to my core.

'Welcome Selina, I have been waiting for you so long my dear!'

✥

Slice

What was I thinking? I shouldn't have started discussing the situation of Rosa's arrival with Jackson when she was questioning Selina's integrity. It took me days to form some kind of friendship with her and in seconds I destroyed everything. I know that she won't trust me now.

Leading Rosa to her allotted chamber, I can't help but wince at the rate she talks. Has she always been this chatty?

Jackson walks beside me stiffly. I don't even know why he is still lingering around. Normally, he would left the minute he would have seen Rosa but today he seems bothered about something.

We reach the third floor, where Rosa would be staying and I move swiftly to open her door. Once she is inside, Jackson, slams the door shut, before dangerously moving towards her.

'Why are you here and what have you done?' he says furiously and I am shocked at his behaviour. Jackson is not this person. What's going on?

'I- I haven't done anything, Jackson.' Rosa says in a high-pitched voice and I know immediately that she has done something.

'I won't repeat my words, Rosa.' Jackson says to which Rosa starts replying something in a low voice but I don't hear anything because at that very moment, I feel a sharp pinch in my spine that whisks my breath away.

Selina is in trouble. I want to say it out loud but the pain crumples me and I can feel the light going away from in front of my eyes.

૪૭

A day later...

Third person

'The war begins tomorrow, and my daughter is nowhere to be found, Jackson. Where is she? Please tell me!' Urusa said, her voice trembling and tears escaping her worried eyes, that were holding down the waterworks ever since the news of her daughter being in danger, apart from being missing, had broken.

Kirst stood by his wife, his hands on her shoulders and his eyes full of despair. He despised the feeling of helplessness that had drawn upon the two of them since his daughter had gone missing. How he wished he could go back in time and keep his family away from this unwanted trouble that had come in the form of a blessing from the Gods.

Blessings were meant to bring joy not constant worry for their only child. But ever since the war had begun, he was just finding a way to keep his child safe. He was angry at the circumstances but even furious at the fact that he could do nothing.

George and Greogina, the heads of the village also stood in the room, their expressions hinted at the fact that they were aware of something, but they didn't say it and no one had the courage to ask them too, after all they were minor Gods and no one wanted their wrath.

'Look Urusa, I have told you repeatedly that I am not aware of anything. I have narrated the whole scene to you multiple times now.' Jackson said, his usual colourful self replaced by a sombre outfit. Rosa was standing behind him, her eyes downcast, a grim expression on her face but something about her body language forced Kirst to think that she was aware of something as well.

The boy, Slice, was sitting in a chair, looking brittle as a glass. He had gone out of his way to form an energy bond with Selina and though Kirst didn't approve of the action he was grateful for his thoughtfulness today. Had he not done that, they would have no way of knowing that Selina was still alive.

If only he could get his daughter back in time before it was too late!

Suddenly, a bright light flashed in the middle of the room causing everyone to step back. A strange serenity started filling everyone's minds which Kirst didn't appreciate but he didn't dare to speak up too! He knew who this was and in these crucial times, the last thing he wanted was to make a God angry.

'Lord Shiva!' Jackson said, bowing down with his hands folded in a namaskar. Everyone else in the room imitated the gesture and closed their eyes to feel the positive aura of the God.

'I am here to assure you that the one you seek will be fine. But I must also warn you, that nothing will be the same anymore. You all will be faced with decisions that you would rather not make but every door you unlock will bring an outcome that's best for you! Slice you will be rewarded for your bravery but it will come at a price that will test your limits. Kirst and Urusa, your daughter shall return soon, my children. George and Greogina, your leadership will be tested in the times to come and Jackson and Rosa, well, you know what you have done. You all still have the time to repent your actions and if you have nothing to repent, I hope you will continue to make the right decisions.' Lord Shiva said before there was a strong burst of light and he disappeared again.

For a minute everyone was smitten. Never had they imagined in their wildest dreams that Lord Shiva would come to personally guide them but here it was, the day they had always secretly prayed for.

'Jackson, Rosa, what was Lord Shiva talking about?' Slice said darkly from his corner, he looked energised like the blessing had already made its way to him.

'Nothing that concerns you Slice, look I must start heading back, I have some work.' Jackson started saying and Rosa nodded her head in approval but Slice stopped them before Kirst could.

'Not so fast, you two. You better start talking or I might have to do something you both would detest.' Slice said while Kirst silently used his magic to create an invisible barrier of Venus Flytraps around Jackson and Rosa. They were his secret weapons that he made everyone believe were extinct.

'How dare you do that to my daughter!' Urusa screamed suddenly. All the distraction had allowed her to enter the minds of Jackson and Rosa and the images she had seen were enough to make her feel like throttling them.

XXXII

Thirty Two

I wake up with bright lights shining on my face. Where am I? My head is spinning, and my legs and hands are bound behind my back. The surface I'm lying on is rough, and my back is starting to hurt as well. As much as I try to recall how I landed in this position, my mind is blank.

The last thing I remember is walking away from Slice, Rosa, and Jackson. I try to look around, but from my current position, my attempts are in vain.

'Oh, look who's finally awake!' A cheerful voice says from afar. Although it feels familiar, I can't quite place it. It's one of those moments when you feel like you should know something, but you can't remember, and it leaves you feeling uneasy.

As the person approaches, my heart rate increases. What if it's an elder's wife or, worse, a Giantess? In my restrained state, the best I can do to defend myself is to head-butt the enemy, but why would she bend down so close to my face?

In a moment, my anxiety is resolved as the person stands in front of me. I could say I'm shocked to see her, but at this point, I'm beyond shocks and surprises. All I can

"]

manage is, "Hello, Gima! How are you doing?"

'It's Gina, not Gima, and you took your own sweet time waking up, didn't you? Was the initial surprise so scary that you couldn't even keep yourself from fainting? Anyway, you should be thankful to your host; she's the one who kept everyone on our team from killing you or hurting you. Otherwise, I don't think you would have woken up to greet me today!' She says with a smirk before bending down to cut the ropes that are keeping me in place.

If she expects me to rush to punch her, she's wrong. All the lessons I've had with Jackson have taught me one thing: to observe my surroundings. I can see the faint buzz of magic around her, forming a protective bubble.

'Are you such a big coward that, even after being free from your bondage, you're going to sit there and do nothing? I must say the Gods have made the best selection for this war.' She says, laughing loudly as if it's the most humorous statement in the world.

'Well, Gima, get rid of the magic bubble first before challenging me, or are you too afraid to stay around me without your magic?' I reply with an innocent smile, which agitates her. She jumps to hit me, but I've already anticipated her move, and I move to the side. She trips on the rock I was tied to and falls flat on her face. The magic protects her from injuries but fails to preserve her pride.

Furious, she gets up with a scream and tries to hit me again, this time with a magic hand, but someone breaks her hand from behind me, making her cry out in pain. Who knew that a damaged magic hand could bring so much pain?

'Learn to follow the instructions, Gina, or next time your punishment will be worse.'

'Maya?' I turn behind immediately to see my ex-mentor standing there. Her hair is bouncy and pink, her dress is long, shiny, and black with no sleeves, and her shoes are silver with the highest heels in the world.

The Maya I knew was all fun and nonchalant, but this Maya is all scary and business despite her pink hair. Her presence here means the war has already begun, as she's part of the enemy troupe. I need to warn the leaders of this infiltration in the building, but how?

'Maya, why are you here? Haven't you done enough damage? Why have you trapped me here?' I say, my voice loud but full of the emotions I felt when she betrayed us.

'You would never understand, Selina, the favor I did for you by staying with you for as long as I did. Anyway, I'm not here to hurt you physically, only to make you remember something you've long forgotten. Then my work here is done. See, I am a good person. Gina, stop crying and tie her back.' she says, tossing her hair back, her voice devoid of emotion.

I look back at Gina, who gives me a glare before performing some magic that binds my hands. The only reason I don't run is that I'm curious to know what they want me to remember so desperately. It also gives me an opportunity to analyze their team dynamics, which may be useful when I escape.

Maya claps twice, and the room fills with various creatures, from nature elements to some members of the elderly. The policemen my aunt had defeated long ago also join the party with scowls on their faces. I make a mental note of everyone in the room.

'Let the movie begin!' Maya screams in a funny accent before sitting down right next to me.

'I hope you enjoy this, Selina, after all, this screening is for you and only you!' Maya whispers to me, making goosebumps rise all over my hands.

A cloud forms in front of us, taking the shape of a rectangle, and the lights slightly dim. A shiver runs down my back as I imagine how helpless I am in this room full of monsters. It's almost like I'm back in the forests of Gionia, and I can only pray that I will escape again unscathed.

The cloud starts turning silver from the corners, and an image slowly starts forming. Suddenly, I hear a crunch from behind, and I look at Maya to confirm if she has heard it too. She indeed has, as she wears an irritated look on her face.

As the image almost finishes forming, I see it—a scene from when I was in Sehar. It looks like one of the early days because of how tiny I am. I shouldn't be more than two years old in the frame, and I start going into shock as I see two strange perturbations on my back that look weirdly like wings. But how is that even possible?

The scene shifts a little, and I realize I'm slightly older, but the wings are even more beautiful now. They are transparent with leaf-like tendrils drawn all over in glittering baby pink and gold. They are so aesthetic and delicate that I feel scared to even look at them for fear of damaging them.

What is Maya showing me? I've never had wings. If I had, the authorities at Sehar would have told my parents, or would they have? After everything that I know about about the royalty now, they would definitely not report such a magical entity to my parents! So the question is if I had them, where did they suddenly disappear? The thought of what might have happened dreads me but I continue to look at the film.

The scene shifts again, and I see myself surrounded by little kids. Rosa stands on the side, tears in her eyes. Jackson stands beside her, holding her tiny hands, a furious look on his face.

"Daddy, why is she special, but I am not?" She sniffles, and he wipes her tears gently before lifting her up.

"Would you be happy, Rose, if she didn't have those wings too?" He asks her lovingly.

I somehow feel like I should have connected the dots earlier that Maya and Jackson are Rosa's parents. My heart fills with a strange sadness as I realize what little Rosa's answer is going to be.

As a tear drips from my eye, the scene changes. The little me stands in darkness, her wings no longer fluttering beautifully. Instead, blood drips from her back, pooling on the ground behind her. Her eyes are full of tears, and her little face is crunched in pain.

"I'm sorry, Selina. That was not my intention," Jackson says, his face apologetic. Rosa stands next to him, tears in her eyes.

The way the scene is structured, I know at the back of my mind that something is amiss, but I know what Maya is trying to do here. She wants to trigger me, and that's the reaction she is going to get. After all, I can act a little like her!

I let out a muffled, angry cry before bending my head to look down at the ground.

'So you see, Selina, they don't really care about you, and they would do anything to keep themselves safe.' Maya says. Gina laughs along with the other monsters as if they all really live for each other and would jump in front of the other to save each other's lives.

'Rosa is your daughter? Why didn't you tell me before?' I say, and Maya's face twitches in anger.

'She is no daughter of mine, neither is she Jackson's. She is Jackson's sister's daughter, but when she was little, for a long time Jackson believed that she was his daughter, and he treated her like a daughter, and still does. My daughter would never make such petty demands, you see; she is powerful on her own!' She says with a smirk.

'Anyways, choose your sides carefully when the time comes.' Maya says, and suddenly I find myself in another room. Is it a hallucination, or is it real? Is that really my mother punching Jackson?

'Ma?' I say before I feel a sharp pain in my head.

XXXIII
Thirty Three

Third Person

Asura fumed in anger as he saw the girl being returned to her world. How dare the spirit disobey his orders? She had been given only one mere task. The blood of the chosen one would have helped him escape straight out of the prison but no, the woman had to make things complicated.

'My Lord, my task is done.' A voice suddenly said. He knew how the woman liked to stay invisible but he recognised her well. After all, she had helped him when he was in his weakest form by creating the rift in the system that had enabled him to get the Giants onboard. He knew she was trying to take advantage of him in her own way, but even if he wasn't in his strongest form yet, he wasn't a fool to let anyone, let alone a conniving woman do that!

'Is your task really done, Maya? You were supposed to end her, yet you could not manage to spill even a single drop of her blood.' He said in a voice that made Maya tremble with fright but she hid her dread well for the monster could have forced her to show herself if he detected her feelings of fear. How he knew her name was an enigma in itself.

'Well, I am playing a long game Lord, you see, even if I didn't spill her blood now, it will spill in the next few hours when she tries to be the hero. Blood spilt in the agony that comes after hope is more powerful, you know that too.' She said trying to convince him of her actions. She didn't like working for him but if it meant getting done with the war more quickly and getting her child back, she would do it gladly.

Maya had somehow managed to convince Jackson that their daughter was safe, but safe was the last thing from the state that she was in. She was a cursed one and no one knew it not even Maya's powerful mother, Mother Nature.

'Fine, go away now, and make sure she diessssss!' Asura screamed, making Maya flinch and disappear quickly.

If the girl didn't die today, he would kill her on his own. He was powerful enough for that now after subtly sucking in the spirit's magic, so much for her thinking she had returned unharmed.

℘

'Selina, is it really you?' My mother says as she pushes away Jackson to run to me. However, two people beat her, my father and Slice. The minute my father reaches me, he envelopes me in a hug and checks me for injuries. Slice quietly stands beside me but I can feel him assessing me too!

'SelSel, where were you and how did you appear out of nowhere?' My mother asks as she finally manages to push my father aside and inspect me.

'Before anything, I must tell you all that the building is infiltrated. Maya, Gina and a few monsters including some elders and the two policemen you threatened last time Aunty are hiding here.' I say and George and Greogina immediately raise their brows for more information. Everyone looks a little shocked as well on seeing my aunt standing amongst them as if they had nearly forgotten about her.

'Ah well, I had sensed them some time back and sent a mind message to these two idiots, if only they would have believed me.' Aunt Yuruslana says to which George makes a weird hmmph-like noise before calling his guards and asking aunt to lead them away.

As Aunt Yuruslana leaves with her little army, George and Greogina leave as well with some guards muttering about making arrangements for the war, and I am left with my parents, Jackson, Rosa and Slice in the room.

'Well Jackson, you were leaving weren't you?' My father says to which he gets an angry glare from my mother but despite his words, Jackson is frozen to his spot.

'Ma I know what Jackson did, Maya showed me a few minutes ago. It was her who had trapped me along with your friend Gina's help Rosa.'- I say looking at Rosa who has the decency to look guilty.-'But I also know that what I was shown wasn't complete, so Jackson I beg you to please tell me the truth. It may be helpful in bringing out the little magic I had in me before you took it away.' I say, my voice heavy with emotions and my heart burning for the damage the little girl suffered.

I know for a fact that Jackson did something to make everyone forget about my wings otherwise, someone would have definitely remembered them over the years.

'What are you all talking about? I feel that we are not on the same page. I thought Jackson and Rosa did something that got you kidnapped but I feel there is more to the story.'

Slice says looking at us and we give a nod.

'Well, it wasn't I who cut your wings, Selina.' Jackson says but before he can talk further, Slice punches him hard on the face.

'You cut her wings, what's wrong with you.' He screams, but before he can attack Jackson further and waste more of our time with getting done with this story, I hold him back.

'Let him talk Slice, we don't have a lot of time on our hands.' I say sternly and he stands back with a frown.

'As I was saying, Rosa wasn't happy with your wings but she wasn't the only one. There were a lot of important people in the capital who had the same thoughts, but where Rosa despised your wings for fame the elders were afraid. I used to think at that time that I was Rosa's father and so I wanted to make her happy but at the same time, I wanted to help you too by keeping you safe. Long story short I was just gonna do a little magic on you that would help you keep your wings hidden in your back instead of parading them everywhere because believe me you hated their weight but someone reached you before us.' Jackson says with tears in his eyes.

'Who did?' My mother asks, her voice so loud that it echoes in the room.

'The King.' Rosa says quietly.

Slice stills beside me, his fists clenched in anger. My parents let out audible gasps and I just can't believe it.

'How can we believe you? What proof do you have and why have you never told me about this before? If you are truthful, you never had a reason to act like criminals and keep the story hidden!' I say my voice quivering with anger.

'Because we had forgotten about it ourselves until Maya returned and reversed the magic. The King had forced Maya to cast a memory spell all over the city, anyone who remembered your wings had forgotten about it until now.' Jackson says his voice heavy with emotions and Rosa nods with a guilty expression.

'Is that the reason you were here Rosa, to warn Jackson, or were you here because you realised your friend Gina is a traitor?' I ask unable to keep the anger out of my voice. I am tired and upset at everyone around me for being so conniving, manipulative and most importantly slow at communicating important information.

Everyone here thinks that they are important and are doing the most important tasks so much so that they keep blaming the one person who knew nothing most of her life for all their miseries.

'Yes, I came here to warn everyone, I was just ashamed of how I trusted in someone who-' Rosa starts saying and I can't help but feel steam coming out of my nose. She is still lying. How can she?

'Rosa, it's better to speak the truth now than spew more lies. I feel that you are working with the enemy and we should imprison you till the end of the war.' Slice says in a grim voice, as if he heard my thoughts, moving forward to capture Rosa but Jackson steps in the middle, shielding her from his grasp.

'Look I can take the responsibility to keep Rosa and her lies away from the others but please don't send her to the chambers.' Jackson says in a pleading voice.

'We can't take those risks anymore Jackson. She brought the enemy home, the war has already begun because of her, we need to put her away before she does more damage.' My mother says in a grim voice before closing her eyes briefly and muttering some words under her breath. I am so engrossed in observing her that I don't even realise what she's done until Jackson gives a little cry.

'No, why did you do that Ursula? I could have brought her back to our side. You didn't have to send her there.' He says, his eyes full of tears.

'Could you have Jackson? She was a liability, if you want to help us, and most importantly help yourself keep your daughter safe, you need to get rid of your baggage.' My mother says in a stern voice.

How did my mother do that? Where did she send Rosa? As much as I am angry at her behaviour, I don't want Rosa to suffer for getting her brain manipulated and filled with nonsense.

'Yursulana has just informed me that she needs help. Slice, Selina you go down and help her. Jackson you are coming with me and Kirst to take charge on the battlefield outside. They are here.' My mother says with a tear in her eyes. As if to confirm her words, we hear a loud thunder followed by a burst of creepy laughter from outside. The chandelier above us shakes before dismantling from the ceiling and falling on the magic bubble that surrounds us. It sparks before disappearing away into the unknown.

Am I capable of this, are we all ready for this? I shiver involuntarily before glancing at Slice who looks a little worried himself. When he looks at me, we know we need to go right away but as we start moving without one last word to my parents or Jackson, my mother pulls me back.

She hugs me tightly before giving me a brief kiss on the forehead.

'Try to stay unharmed till we come to rescue you.' She whispers into my ear before releasing me. Her words bring out a sob I didn't know I was holding back, but I control it before it becomes worse.

My father hugs me too, gently caressing my hair, tears flowing from his eyes as he looks at me one last time before we hopefully meet again.

As my parents move to greet Slice, I go to Jackson, who is standing there with a stoic face.

'You will take care of them, please Jackson, if anything starts going wrong, you will find a way to signal me. You have to promise Jackson.' I say grabbing his hands which are cold as ice as he stands there without saying a word.

I look at him with hope in my eyes, till Slice comes to take me away. As Slice leads me from the room, I hear a choked voice of Jackson-'I promise you, Selina!' And they are gone too, my parents and my teacher.

For a moment, we just stand there, two teenagers thrust into a war that they want to run away from but then we hear an explosion and like a snap of fingers we come out of our heads and start running towards the source.

XXXIV

Thirty Four

Smoke fills the right-hand side of the corridor, making it impossible to look at anything beyond the black clouds. The once thick, white ceilings, now look like a plot straight out of a dreaded castle. As the smoke progresses, a nasty smell starts drifting towards us.

Slice mutters some words and a pink protection bubble forms around us. He holds my hand and with a nod, we start walking towards the smoke. As soon as it touches the bubble, sparks generate, showing how dangerous it is, but we keep moving on under our shield. How useful am I going to be in this magical fight?

We move down the hallway, cautiously taking every step to avoid getting killed by a monster in the shadows. While Slice keeps chanting some mantras, I look out for anything out of the ordinary that we might need to eliminate before moving on.

As we reach the stairs we need to take in order to reach the basement, we see the source of the smoke. A flaming black mass sits there, body hidden under a hideous robe that is covered in little centipedes making me feel like throwing up. For a minute, I think it's the bleeding man but my worries are evaporated when Slice mutters its name.

'Dhumavati, goddess of smoke, why is she sitting here in this form?' He whispers, his voice trembling.

'Is she scary?' I ask with curiosity, having never heard her name before. Her posture alludes to mystery and creates a frenzy in my heart.

'Normally, people are scared of her, she is not one of the Goddesses that spread a lot of optimism but I have heard that she is kind-hearted and maybe if we speak to her, we can get to know her intentions and bring her back to our side.' Slice whispers and hope fills my heart.

'Goddess Dhumavati, is that you? I bow before you in greetings Goddess.' Slice whispers before bowing down with his hands folded in a namaskar. I copy his gesture and immediately bow down too.

'Children of my sworn enemy, unfortunately, your gestures do not bring me peace. I need to end you to leave this place and go back home. It's not my time yet you know to be present on Earth.' She says, her voice cracking a little signalling her old age and her body trembling out of an emotion that I can't make out.

'Goddess, why have you decided to side with the enemy, we really need your assistance in these hard times. Please take mercy and help us put the monsters back in the cells.' Slice says with his head bowed but suddenly out of nowhere a cloud of smoke hits him hard in the chest despite the shield and he falls back coughing violently.

'I said, I can't help you! Haven't you humans disrespected me enough over the years?' She screams, a waft of black smoke coming out of her mouth.

At first, I am scared but then I close my eyes and see the faces of my parents and all those who are fighting today. I have to do something to help them- help Aunt Yuruslana, who is fighting down there alone with a few people on her side.

'Goddess I know that the pain you have felt over the years is unsurmountable, but I request you to please not give up on the goodwill of your heart. It is an established fact that humans are not the wisest creatures in the universe, how else would they have lost everything on the planet, so please, help us attain victory and save the lives of those who would suffer unnecessarily if the monsters win.' I say, my voice soft and barely audible but my words strong and succinct.

For a moment nothing happens and only a thick black fog starts filling up the space but then the smoke starts lifting up and the Goddess changes form. The centipede-filled robes disappear and she appears in the form of a clean old lady with tattered clothes.

'You have provoked my kindness with your words. Go and help your friends.' She says before moving aside. I can't believe how easily she agreed to change sides. Slice was correct when he said that she is a kind Goddess.

I remove the big coat I am wearing and after checking the pockets for anything important, lay it in front of the Goddess who is now standing on a side, her arms crossed in front of her.

'Goddess, I don't have much to offer you but please accept this coat from my back. It will keep you warm and protected for a long time.' I say humbly with my hands folded and I am lost for words when I see a single tear fall from the goddess's eye.

'You are indeed unique Selina, I will be there to assist you when you transform.' She says before disappearing into thin air.

'What happened?' Slice says coughing from behind me, still on the floor, the impact of the smoke being stronger than it appeared initially. Rushing to his aid, I help him up slowly as I repeat the events from before.

'I really can't believe that you convinced the Goddess but you are indeed a different force Selina.' He says, before coughing some more and then standing tall on his own.

'C'mon, we need to hurry now. I can sense our team losing.' Slice says before running down the steps as I trail behind him.

As we get closer to the war zone, the smell of blood and sweat fills the air. It is a mixture of coppery, salty and suffocating, like a place you run away from not towards.

We are about to climb down the last step when suddenly Slice stops in front of me making me crash into him. He holds me behind with one hand as he looks around carefully. Once or twice he flutters his left hand's fingers in front of us and when he is done doing whatever he is doing, he makes me climb back a few steps and counts to three.

I am prepared for everything but what happens next. A magical shield that I had not witnessed earlier starts glowing as far as I can see from my position. It then trembles and thunders a few times before bursting with a loud crackling sound that makes me jump a little.

'That was Maya's trap. Anyone who bumps into it would find themselves in an unknown place so horrible that they would be wishing for death. Maya had used this magic once when Jackson had just rescued me and we were running from a creature of strange heritage. She was on the good side momentarily, I wonder if she brought back the creature now that she is evil again.' Slice says as we watch the last of the magic wall burn away.

'It's good that the wall was just created otherwise it would have taken longer to destroy it. But let's hurry now, if Maya made that wall it means she is onto something horrible.' Slice says and I can't help but feel anxious to end it all quickly before the psycho woman hurts innocents.

We run towards the sound of fighting, the bubble that Slice had made around us now also keeping us hidden from plain sight. As we move closer, we see an unfair fight in progress. The men from Greog fight to keep themselves alive as the turned spirits and witch-like people kick them around like a ball. I see my aunt fighting alone with Maya, Gina and one other monster and can't help but feel enraged at the sight.

As furious as I am, I also can't help but feel proud of my aunt for dealing with three enemies at once. Slice mutters some words next to me and suddenly Gina turns into a flower. Maya gives out a shriek on seeing her and the monster- who looks like a mix between a human and a cactus- looks confused.

Slice mutters a few more words and the monster also turns into a flower. As Maya gets distracted by Slice's creations, my aunt uses the opportunity to set her on fire.

She screams loudly, gaining the attention of her army most of whom don't look so confident seeing their leader burning away.

My aunt mutters a few more words and the next thing I see is Maya and her army locked in metal cages, banging at the doors, trying their best to get away.

The minute all the enemies in the room are trapped, a shining cloud forms in a corner and Swarn steps out.

'Thank you Yuruslana and Slice, I will take care of these evils now. You need to hurry though, the war outside has started in full swing and your side doesn't seem to be doing so well. Selina, remember always, you are blessed.' Swarn says with a smile on his face before turning to look at the cages in dismay. He swings his hands around and a second later, the only people left in the room are my aunt, her men, Slice and I.

XXXV

Thirty Five

'Thank you children for reaching here on time. I don't know how long we would have been able to stay alive without your aid.' My aunt says with a cough, as she sits down to regain her breath. It's then that I see blood coming out of her nose. Slice notices it too and we rush beside her.

The soldiers don't look so good either. Being tossed around like footballs, many of them are clutching their hands or legs in pain, with blood seeping down from their injuries. Some of them are also wondering around looking dazed and confused. Slice mutters some words again and they all shout words of joy as their injuries get cured.

'Aunt Yuruslana, you need rest. Unfortunately, I can't cure your injury as it's a side effect of using too much magic for vengeance.' Slice says and I can't help but feel despair.

'I can't rest boy, you know that. They need us outside. I will fight to my death if I have to.' Aunt Yuruslana says making me feel emotional. It's true that I always felt scared of her in the past but in the last few days, she protected me like a mother. She also took care of everyone here in Greog. She is an essential member of the tribe who needs to survive the war.

'Aunt Yuruslana, you can't talk about death. Please regain your energy before coming outside. Trust me, we will do our best to keep everyone alive till you return.' I say, trying to reassure her and she smiles.

'Selina, I know you think you are not special but you are my dear. You just need to believe in yourself more you know.' She says before closing her eyes and suddenly falling asleep.

'Is she alright? What happened?' I ask panicked.

'Don't worry, I have put her to sleep for a while. She needs it. Let's go now, Jackson just linked me, it's getting bad out there.' Slice replies with his teeth clenched in anxiety.

We leave a few soldiers to take care of Aunt Yuruslana and run outside with the remaining. If what we saw inside earlier was scary, the sight we see outside is like a nightmare.

Giants of every kind raise havoc as our little army tries to fight back. People including children lie dead in every direction, as blood from their injuries seeps through the ground.

On one end, I see my parents fighting a huge Giant that looks like the King from the way he wears a crown on his head. As I squint my eyes, I realise it is the same Giant I had seen in my dream. Praying for my parents' safety I turn around to see George and Greogina fighting two other Giants nearby causing alot of smoke to rise up from the fire they keep extinguishing from the Giants' attack.

Thunder rings in the air as I look up to see Jackson fighting a Giant that looks like a dreadful mix of a Vulture and a Crocodile. What even are these combination Giants?

The buildings that made up the village are nowhere in sight, instead, all that's left of them are the broken bits and pieces that litter the ground like construction trash. A beautiful village burns through the fires of war all because of the Giants and their master.

Suddenly the air around me flickers and I watch Slice mesmerised as he single-handedly kills a couple of 'ethical' Giants, that were fighting some human soldiers, with his magic. They fall like dominoes one after the other, causing a tremble through the ground due to their weight. The soldiers run away to save themselves from getting crumpled by the Giants' weight.

As the Giants fall, so does Slice and I hurry to catch him. Blood rushes out of his nose, and he shivers from how weak the magic makes him.

'Slice, just take some of my energy, we need you!' I say to him but he shakes his head.

'No Selina, I won't do that. I just need some time.' He whispers, his voice barely audible over the chaos.

Suddenly, a wind passes us and Slice disappears. I look around in panic until I catch a glimpse of the wind monster running away with Slice as Slice tries to put up a fight against him.

The Giant has long silvery hair and a slim-toned body. He is dressed in animal skin and has red slits for eyes. He holds Slice in his fist like a toy he hates. When the Giant sees me, he gets a malicious smile on his face. He rushes towards me and as I prepare to fight he passes from above me whispering taunts like lullabies.

'Poor girl, the chosen one. How will you protect your friends? You are nothing without the boy's magic.' He says, laughing loudly at the end of each sentence. His laugh sounds like he is about to sneeze but he feels proud of it.

'Is that how you fight? I don't even know your name, pity. The Giant King had sent us a list of names of the warriors he thought were worthy but he forgot to mention yours so can you please tell me your name.' I say loudly, mustering as much courage as I can, as he rushes past me a second time and my words bring him to a halt.

'You got a list? Lies, I don't believe it for a second. I am the King's advisor. He wouldn't fail to mention such an idiocy to me.' He says, losing the hold on Slice in his outrage. Slice falls on the ground with a humph and quickly hides behind a log to stay out of sight of the Giant while he chants some mantras.

'Well, well, the reason you think it an idiocy is why the King kept you out of the loop. He knew that if you were involved, you would prove to be a hindrance to a task so trivial and thus, he got it done so veiled that you didn't even get a murmur about it.' I say confidently as the Giant falls for every word and gets an offended, melancholic look on his face.

'Ahh, that Rakshasa, he thinks he can hide things from me, Va, the blessed devotee of Vayu. Just because he has Asura's support he thinks he is high and mighty. The minute this war ends, I will challenge him. But first, I need to end you. Wait where are you? What's wrong with my eyes?' He screams as Slice throws my sword towards me. Where was he carrying it all this while? I catch the little beauty and run towards the Giant, stabbing it in his stomach with as much ferocity as possible.

The Giant screams for a minute, the air around him wooshing as he loses control of it. After a minute of suffering, he falls to the ground with a thump. The ground quivers from the impact of such a huge creature falling and Slice and I struggle to maintain balance and not fall flat on our faces.

After a few minutes, the vibrations stop and the winds blow away leaving behind the huge dead body of the Giant. Suddenly a golden glow covers the Giant's body and rises above till it becomes smaller and smaller and ultimately disappears in the sky.

'That was Va's magic. Whenever a person with magic dies, either the magic from the body goes into the inheritor or disappears into the sky in the absence of one. Let's go now and help our team with other enemies.' Slice says and turns to walk towards the war but I somehow can't move. Every time I have killed a Giant either I have run away or woken up in a different place, this time as I take in my actions I feel guilty of being a murderer and don't feel quite right about leaving the body to get rotten.

Seeing that I have not moved from my place, Slice comes to join me and in the unsaid conversation that flows between us, he somehow understands what I feel.

Muttering a few words, he uses his magic to cover the Giant's body with a thin white sheet and it is only then that I feel at peace.

Whispering a soft thank you to Slice and a few prayers for the Giant, I turn back, feeling stronger about facing the other Giants. We wait a few minutes, as Slice closes his eyes in meditation to gain his energy back, all the while muttering words of apology and as if the Gods of magic see his good deeds, he starts looking like himself in no time. His new found energy, makes me feel fresh too and we move ahead.

We walk slowly but steadily towards the raging war, keeping a lookout for any horrorful surprises as well as analysing the areas that need our help. Squinting my eyes, I see a dreadful scene in front of me. A worm-like Giant corners a little child, ready to swallow it using its huge tongue. As the child panics and tries to escape, the tongue slithers towards him like a snake.

Without thinking further, I start running towards the child, Slice in tow, muttering words to destroy any shields in our way. The tongue almost touches the boy when I grab hold of him and pull him away. The tongue narrowly misses the little child but hits me on the back making me hiss in the burning pain. As I fall on the ground unable to bear the pain that spreads like flames all over my back, I vaguely hear the giant fall on the ground dead.

The child holds my hand with a smirk on his little face covered with dirt and its only then that I realise it was a trap. Asura tightens his hold on me, his little hands choking me despite being nowhere near my throat.

As I almost give up, I look at his face reflecting victory and joy. At a distance I see my parents struggling to keep up with Rakshasa's attacks. He suddenly does some spell and I see Papa flying away and hitting his back on a tree, and that's when I lose my mind. How dare this monster hurt my father who is the most wonderful man in this world, who is full of kindness and love, who would do anything to protect the ones he cares about?

A sudden need for revenge burns through me and a fire burns through my blood. No longer do I feel the choking grasp of Little Man, all I feel is the desire to burn him back to his prison in hell. His eyes widen once he realises something is wrong with me and he tries to get away but this time I hold him with all my might till I feel a shriek coming out of my throat as my back rips causing a loud explosion around me and my eyes close on their own.

XXXVI

Epilogue

Third Person

'I can't believe what happened three days back. It's impossible what she did.' Greog said pacing around, worry etched on his face. Magic always had consequences. When someone used it maliciously, it laid a curse on them unbeknownst to many, when someone used it in vengeance, it made them weak with every spell cast.

To use such a powerful spell and still live was a miracle on its own and it scared Greog beyond his wits. It was like living a nightmare.

'She did it Greog and it's high time you start believing it. The Gods helped us indirectly when they saw us fighting bravely. They showed their presence through her and destroyed all our enemies in a go.' Greogina said as she fixed the last of the village with her magic.

The people living in the building thanked her from afar before moving inside their houses and alas Greog and Greogina were left all alone staring at their beloved village that had miraculously survived the Giant attack all because of a teenager.

Whispering a thank you to the Gods and reciting a small prayer to keep them protected from the unknown dangers that were coming their way, Greog and Greogina returned back to their place.

'She has wings.' Whispered a voice into Rosa's ears.

'She is famous again Rosa, while you lie here locked up all because of the girl's mother.' Whispered the tormenting voice again.

Ever since she had been sent here, Rosa felt like she was back in Thornos. The torment never stopped, it drove her crazy. Why did she have to always be the one siding with the evil? If only someone could release her out.

'Selina, you are in grave danger now, I can feel it. Asura won't stop, he will return.' Slice whispered as he sat beside Selina in the medical room. He felt like half the time she had been in the village she had only been in this room.

'Slice, I will learn to use my wings again and I promise we will be better prepared for the next time. But first, we need to do something important.' She whispered back as he knelt down to listen to what she wanted.

Selina's parents looked at the scene unfold from the door, grateful for their child being safe but worried about how they would keep her protected now that her powers had finally been unleashed. The war was far from over and they prayed with all their heart that their little family would survive to tell the tale.

&

'How dare they trick me like that? Keep me from tasting victory, I will not be stoppeddddd!' Asura screamed in his mind as he was brought back to hell in the state he was in when he had just signed a pact with the foolish Giants.

'My Lord, at last, I have found you. It was difficult but nothing could stop me. Don't worry, I will help you now and then together we will rule the world.' The feminine voice said, laughing hysterically. As Asura recognised her, a pride reflected in his soul. She had found him alas, his most trusted weapon had escaped. Nothing will stop him now from ending the world, Gods' chosen one or not!

OTHER WORKS

Selina has ended here but the story hasn't.

Rosa, the sequel is coming soon to your favorite stores! Follow my Instagram to stay updated.

Some of my other work:

- Novels:

    ◦ That Night At The Hotel
    ◦ Lost Stars

- Poetry Book:

    ◦ Thoughts in my Mind

Note: All my books are available now on Amazon, Flipkart(India), Barnes and Noble and Notion Press apart from 30000+ other platforms

www.ingramcontent.com/pod-product-compliance
Lightning Source LLC
Chambersburg PA
CBHW021435150726
47989CB00001B/263